Lethal Complications

by

David O'Neil

Argus Enterprises International, Inc.
New Jersey***North Carolina

A-Argus Better Book Publishers, LLC

For information:
A-Argus Better Book Publishers, LLC
9001 Ridge Hill Street
Kernersville, North Carolina 27285
www.a-argusbooks.com

ISBN: 978-0-6156428-2-6
ISBN: 0-6156428-2-9

Book Cover designed by Dubya
Printed in the United States of America

Chapter One

Jonathon Glynn strolled along the quay at Boulogne. There were several boats moving in the yacht harbour, and for a moment, he didn't recognise the *Swallow* motoring in to a berth alongside the next pontoon. The tall figure on the stern of the ketch called out to the helm, unseen by Jonathon. "Stop! Whenever you like would be good." He then edged two big fenders over the stern to cushion the impact as the boat moored stern-to. Despite the rude remarks that were just audible from below, the actual impact of boat and pontoon was gentle.

"So what brings you two back to the Republic? Should I open the armoury? Perhaps let your parents know? Or is it purely social?"

Donny Weston looked up in surprise. "Jonathon? What are you doing here? The last we heard you were deeply involved in wooing the fair Carol."

Jonathon flushed, "Just leave my fiancée out of this conversation......"

"Fiancée! Abby, here quick. Jonathan has popped the question already."

Abby Marshall suddenly appeared from the depths of the cockpit. "Jonathon who?"

Seeing the figure standing on the pontoon, she shrieked, "Jonathon, why haven't you told anyone? Where is she?"

Jonathon laughed. "Hold on. Carol is in Paris. I was just visiting the town on business. I certainly did not expect to see you. After all it has been three months since we left you in the south of France, and you were using the RV at the time."

Donny laughed. "We have just returned from Gran Canarias. We picked up the boat from Cobh and took the folks to Las Palmas for a holiday. They are flying home. We came here to recover the RV and pay a visit to the cousins who are studying at the Sorbonne. Abby has a cousin there and so do I."

"Will you need the apartment?"

"No thanks," said Abby. "We enjoy using the RV. We booked a campsite on the internet so we can be independent. Thanks anyway. Come below and I'll feed you. We are both starving and I've created a huge stew."

Jonathon laughed. "No, thank you. I have already eaten. Anyway, I must go back to my meeting, I have already stayed away too long. If you are still here tonight I will see you then. If not, perhaps Paris?" He turned and strode off along the pontoon, and back along the quay.

Abby ducked down into the cabin and came up with her cell phone. Without hesitation, she stabbed a speed-dial number. Jonathon's blackberry shivered. "Yes?"

"You have company. Two people, grey anorak and blue zip jacket with Breton hat."

"Interesting! Thanks for the heads-up." Jonathon rang off, then pressed a speed-dial number of his own.

On the boat Donny lifted an eyebrow at Abby. She shrugged."You know Jonathon. I was just making sure. Let's eat. I'm starving." She went below. Donny glanced around the area then joined her.

The couple were relaxed with each other. Both were in their nineteenth year, fit and athletic. They were enjoying a gap year in their University studies. They had, over the past few months, been involved in a very nasty fracas with a Paris-based criminal organization. It had been the culmination of nearly three years of trouble with the organization. Only now were they able to relax a little without the threat of an imminent attack. The final showdown had been less than two months ago, and had resulted in a shootout with the gang. Donny and Abby had survived. The whole business had brought them closer together.

Jonathon Glynn was a member of the security services at the Embassy in Paris. He was a close friend and support throughout the entire episode.

As she served out the steaming stew onto two big soup-plates, she asked casually, "Watchers?"

"Just the one, over beside the café. I think he detached from Jonathon's team." He took his plate, a piece of bread and a spoon and went up to the cockpit, where he was joined by Abby. The pair sat in the sun eating, and keeping an eye on their watcher.

"I see he has found a friend."Abby observed. Do you think we should worry?"

"Let's go up to town after lunch, I think a little more formally dressed perhaps."

Donny glanced at Abby's bikini top and brief shorts.

He received a slap for his comment and they went below laughing to dress for town.

Jonathon had been collected by arrangement, leaving his followers bewildered by his disappearance. The team, dropped off by the battered painter's van that collected him, took up the chase of his former followers.

Abby's phone vibrated just as they entered the Printemps store. She stopped to take the call just outside on the street. Donny whisked her out of the way as the errant motor cycle roared onto the pavement scattering people left and right. The rider regained control, got back on the roadway and disappeared round the corner with a roar of his exhaust.

"Phew. That was a near thing," Donny said. "Who was on the phone?"

"No one," Abby said. "I mean, it was a wrong number. A voice said 'goodbye' and rang off."

"Odd, don't you think?" Donny said quietly. "Lucky I was here and saw that bike coming. Come on now. We have things to buy." He urged Abby through the glass doors into the store.

While Abby was in the changing room trying on several dresses, Donny rang Jonathon. He mentioned Abby's narrow escape. "Do you have any ideas, Jonathon?"

"I hate to say this, but it could be your connection with me. Stay with the crowds and I'll call you back later." He rang off. Donny turned to see Abby coming out of the changing room, followed by a slim dark-haired woman. Abby avoided looking at Donny, which warned him that something was wrong. He made his way to the entrance to the department ahead of the pair. As Abby reached the door, with a muttered apology, Donny rammed the man in front of him into the woman behind Abby. She fell over, revealing the gleam of the knife she had been holding at Abby's back. Donny went to assist the fallen woman, managing to tread on her hand in the process, and causing her to release her grip on the knife. He stood, kicking the knife away and apologised to the woman.

From behind, he heard Abby say, "Put her down, man, you're already spoken for."

He swung round and collected her in his arms. "Abby, darling, how lovely to see you here." Tucking her arm under his, he took her off to the coffee bar in the store. The dark-haired woman had gone, lost in the swirl of the people in the busy store.

Donny called a cab and they returned to the boat. There Donny opened the concealed panel and took out two of the automatics, plus magazines. He relocked the panel and passed one of the guns to Abby, along with a full magazine. They each stripped their gun and reassembled it, slotting the loaded magazine in place.

Jonathon arrived as they were having coffee after eating their evening meal. The dinghy puttered alongside. With much laughter and chat, the occupant was invited on board for a drink. There was activity on many of the boats in the marina around them, music and laughter in the soft summer air.

Jonathon could tell them little. "We traced the headquarters of the people who were following me, but it turned out to be a detective agency, briefed to follow an errant husband, me." He paused, "Whoever followed you two was not part of the detective agency brief.

There is a possibility that, the contract that was out on you before, has been renewed, though by whom I have no idea."

"I wonder what they want. It might help if we knew who they were."

Jonathon ventured, "The other possibility is that you have been recognized as the two people who wiped out the Merry Jordon gang* [Fatal Meeting by David O'Neil].

That being the case someone may well think you are on the track of someone else in the business and they are just eliminating what they consider a threat."

"Such a reassuring assessment of our current situation, Jonathon. What are you talking about? Neither of us was associated officially with the Jordon business. The people who were aware must also have known that we were only dragged into things by accident. So, tell us; what are you involved in that has made us targets once more?"

Abby and Donny both looked at Jonathon with interest as he sat and worked out how much or little he should tell them.

He said, "Nothing goes out of this cabin! By the way, you may be committing yourselves to a situation that could cause you considerable harm."

The two youngsters exchanged looks, and in unison they nodded.

"There is a movement afoot to control the way the EU is managed." Jonathon paused, thinking. "The Brussels bureaucracy is a huge pot of influence and interest. It generates rules and spends money with very little control from the Governments that created it. The civil service created has attracted the talents of the best and worst of the member states.

"What should have been a benevolent service has become the target for the criminal and the venal, and while some good things are still done, they are mainly now a cover, a diversion, for the bad.

"My part is the investigation of criminal intrusion into the whole mess. So far I have found evidence of activity from the USA and China, criminal activity from Germany, France, and Britain, and I have no doubt the list will grow longer. The Arab nations are still keeping a low profile, though I suspect they are funding the efforts, of some of the existing participants."

He sat back and looked at the two people on the opposite side of the table. "This is big time. Billions are involved. Take my advice and turn this boat around, head for the other side of the Earth. I really do not want your deaths on my conscience."

Donny looked at Abby. "Perhaps it would be a good idea. After all we really don't know who we are facing here." He stood but tripped over Jonathon's foot. Both Jonathon and Abby bent to help him up. The spatter of glass was the only warning that someone had shot at the trio through the cabin window. Donny's fall had saved them all from injury.

Abby stabbed the light switch dowsing the lights. Jonathon ducked through the cabin door into the cockpit of the ketch. All three had guns in their hands as they crouched searching for the origin of the silenced rounds.

Donny slid over the bow onto the foredeck of the boat moored beside them as Jonathon rolled off the stern onto the pontoon. Abby, with gun up, searched the area in the general direction of the shooter.

There was no sign of movement or, in fact, of anything out of the ordinary. The shattered glass was the mute reminder that the shooting had occurred.

They found no sign of the shooter. The broken glass was cleared up and the window taped over. The bullets had lodged in the woodwork just missing the upholstered back cushions of the port side seat. It was clear the gun had been fired from a low elevation, somewhere across the Marina.

Jonathon had been over the other side searching. There was one spot where someone had smoked several cigarettes. He guessed they were Chinese, despite them being marked with a famous English brand name. He pointed out where the nicotine staining was excessive. "That normally would not happen on the milder, legal British varieties. The Chinese forgeries are made with dangerously high levels of nicotine and other harmful chemicals."

"So, are we any further forward, Jonathon?"

"Only that we now have proof that you are regarded as a threat by some Chinese group. In view of this, I do urge you to shove off and remove the threat to your lives."

After making arrangements for the repair of the broken window in the cabin of *Swallow,* Donny and Abby left her in the charge of the boatyard. They put their bags in a hire car and departed the marina in the early hours of the following day. Making sure they were not followed, they managed to reach the RV in her garage without detection.

Abby took the hire car to the airport and left it with the agent there, taking the shuttle bus back to Boulogne. She rejoined Donny in the RV and both adopted the disguises they had selected. For Abby the brunette wig and the dark-rimmed glasses changed her look which, when added to the knee-length pencil skirt in black with the white cotton blouse, gave her the appearance of a professional lawyer or accountant.

For Donny the shirt and tie; with blazer and slacks, combined with the pony tail wig, replacing his bleached short crop. The difference, while not so marked, was enough in Abby's estimation. The sun-glasses completed the ensemble, but as both insisted, only for when they were in civilization.

They travelled armed all the time, especially when they were in public places.

The next incident occurred when they were strolling, arms round each other, in the marsh country of the south. The area was covered in the scrub bushes that grew in the wetland ground. The track was raised slightly above the water level, part of the pattern of communicating ways connecting the bull-breeding and horse-breeding farms that defined the area. The hazy sun was warm. They had parked on a site located in the Camargue near the small village of

Villeneuve. They were dressed casually, feeling fairly relaxed.

Three men in suits appeared on the track, ahead of them. There were no other people in sight. All three were casually carrying small machine pistols with stick magazines. Donny and Abby stopped. Donny took hold of Abby's Walther, tucked into the small of her back. Abby took a grip on Donny's. The three men drew closer and Donny raised his hand to stop them, shouting, "You are making a mistake. We have no interest in what you do, or who you are. Please do not shoot us."

In answer the nearest man laughed tauntingly and raised his gun and sprayed several bullets in the road in front of the two youngsters.

"Close enough," Abby said quietly. "Now!"

The two separated, going either side of the track. As they moved, both thumbed the safety catch off and opened fire on the three men. The shooter died where he stood. The others were much more wary. Both dived to the verges and opened fire. The result was bullets flying everywhere. Accuracy was not guaranteed with the mini guns. Abby fired a second time, aiming at the place where her target had found cover. She was cool and calm, prepared to select her shots. After their experiences of the past two years when they had been involved in a battle to the death with a French gang, both she and Donny had been prepared to defend themselves. Donny called from his position. "OK, Abby? "

Abby fired at a twitch on the grass at about the right place and answered. "I'm fine, I think I may have pinked mine. How about you?"

The man on Abby's side of the track chanced a quick look. Abby fired. He reared up, dropped his gun and gasped as Abby's shot took him in the neck. Both hands went to try to stop the suddenly-spurting blood.

Donny was hugging the ground as his opponent kept firing short bursts to keep him under pressure. Abby looked across but she could only see a small stretch of leg, and that moved out of sight just as she looked.

She called to Donny, as she slotted a new magazine into the butt of her automatic, "I can see him. I'll distract him. Get ready."

Donny shouted, "No. Don't take the chance..."

As he said it, he was half rising. Abby rose her feet, blazing away at the spot where the last gunman was lying. The man started up, swinging the mini gun towards the girl. Two of her shots hit him in the chest. Donny's shot shattered the mini gun with a hit on the mechanism. The man dropped the gun, and collapsed moaning to the ground.

Donny kicked the remains of the gun away from the wounded man. Abby came across and the couple exchanged looks just to be sure the other was unwounded.

Donny ran his hand over the man and retrieved an automatic, and a wallet. The ID card revealed that the holder was Chinese/French named Che Wan. There was over ten thousand euro's and a picture of a lady in a cheongsam dress. The man looked at the pair with a blank expression on his face. Abby looked at his wounds. She glanced at Donny and almost imperceptibly shook her head.

The wounded man spoke suddenly. "They didn't say you would be armed. They said it would be easy." He coughed and blood leaked from the corner of his mouth.

"Why?" Donny asked. "Why were you trying to kill us?"

The man looked surprised. "He thinks you have the secret."

"What gave him that idea, I wonder?" Donny said wondering who 'he' was.

"I am not going to make it, am I?" The man whispered.

Abby said quietly, "No, I think not."

Che Wan nodded slowly, "Please email my wife in picture. Say sorry, from me. Isobel tell boss about you....."

He stopped suddenly. Dead!

Donny looked at Abby swiftly. "Let's get the hell out of here." They each looked around to see if anyone was showing interest in the gun battle that had just occurred. There was no one to be seen. Abby produced a plastic carrier bag from her handbag and packed the two working mini guns with the wallets of the three dead men inside. Donny dragged the bodies off the track and into the marshy land on the other side of some bushes.

The bloodstains were covered with dust kicked over the spots by Abby. Donny finished off hiding the bodies in the marsh where they began to sink into the ground even as he worked. He threw the shattered mini gun into the marsh with the bodies.

They made their way back to the campsite, where Abby put the working guns into the armoury concealed under the floor of the RV.

The wallets of the three men revealed little. All were Chinese citizens of France. They shared the same address in Paris. All had money, the leader, Che Wan, carried over ten thousand euro's, the others five thousand plus each. Abby looked at the photograph, which was the only personal thing found apart from the driving licences. On the reverse were some words she could not understand, and an email address.

She showed Donny.

"When we get to an internet café, I think." Donny said thoughtfully. "What do you think?"

"I think so." Abby replied and kissed him on the cheek.

Donny looked at her, startled. "What was that for?"

"Are you complaining?" Abby teased...

"No, of course not..." he didn't finish because he couldn't. Abby trapped him against the table, and kissed him firmly and comprehensively on the lips, pressing her body against him. It was late afternoon by the time they came up for air.

Still lying on the bed, Abby said, "I'd be happier if we changed our location. Parked somewhere else for the night. What do you think?"

"I agree, but first I think I'll dig out Jonathon's gadget. I still don't know how they found us.

During the events of the prior year when they were involved with Harry Sanders, successor to Merry Jordan as leader of the gang, Jonathon had given them a 'bug' sniffer. A little electronic detector which Donny quickly dug out of the armoury. The RV had been a gift from Jonathon, who had picked it up in a government surplus sale. Designed as a surveillance and headquarters vehicle, it looked innocent, just another commercial RV; it had hidden features. These included carbon-fiber lining to protect users from gunfire, a built in armory, plus a satellite communication system.

The detector started flashing immediately as it was switched on. The bug was attached to the chassis under the rear tow-bar. Donny took the bug and walked round the village to the café where, finding a car with a Lyon number plate, he stuck the bug under the bumper and came back to the RV where Abby waited. She started up at his nod and drove off along the D37 to Nimes.

David O'Neil

Chapter Two

In Paris, Jonathon was being addressed by his boss. He always thought that people who spoke at public meetings should keep their PA voice for such occasions. His boss seemed to find it impossible to speak at less than a shout. "Bring them in," shouted Hillary Walker, head of the M16 station in Paris. "We cannot have these young people cavorting around the Continent bringing mayhem to our French allies."

"With respect, Director, they are not the normal irresponsible people you may associate with other people of their age group." He held up his hand to stop the immediate reply. "These two youngsters have proved over the past two years that they have the sense and abilities to look after themselves. In addition, I have no ideas where they are. Finally any attempt to restrain them for their own good—or otherwise—could be embarrassing for the Department and would be opposed vehemently."

"We are discussing two eighteen-year-olds, are we not?"

Jonathon marvelled at the foghorn voice.

"In which case this discussion is over. Pick them up and hold them for their own protection. Do you understand me?"

Jonathon nodded, "If I can find them, I will."

Exasperated, she finished, "Just find them!"

The portly figure of Hillary Walker strode off, her back still rigid with indignation at the temerity of Jonathon Glynn. *Just like a spook, they think they know it all.* She would soon have them sorted out.

Jonathon, on the other hand, was thinking that for someone who had been appointed only two weeks ago she had a lot to learn.

The SAT phone beeped as the RV cruised along the road north from Nimes. Abby answered. "Hullo, JG. What's new?"

"I have been instructed to pull you in for your own protection. So would you care to come home and set yourselves up in a safe house where we can protect you properly?"

"In a word. No!"

"Why am I not surprised? Keep your heads down, whatever. The people involved in this affair are truly nasty."

"Thanks for the tip off. By the way, does the name 'Isobel' mean anything in this present context?"

"Where did that come from?"

Abby explained about the bug and the incident in the Camargue, finishing with the last few words of Che Wan.

Jonathon said, "Have you sent an email off?"

"No, we haven't found an internet café yet."

"Don't. Give me the email address."

Abby read it out. Jonathon rang off.

"Well, did he have any suggestion to make?"

"Just to come in out of the way, so that the service could deal with the matter and keep us safe whilst so doing." Abby giggled, "How about that?" She said in her most pompous voice

Donny laughed and negotiated a bend in the road, avoiding a parked car.

"Oh, oh, we have a tail." He watched the car they had just passed take up a position behind them.

Abby went to the rear of the RV. There was no window there but there was a viewing panel that allowed a view of the road behind with added advantage of enlarging the picture to identify faces in a trailing car.

"Pull over at the next lay-bye, Donny. It's Jonathon."

The rest area beside the road had plenty of parking room for the RV and the Peugeot driven by Jonathon. He joined them as soon as he had parked the car.

Abby had the coffee on and the three sat around the table while Jonathon debriefed them exhaustively about the incidents they had dealt with since their last meeting.

He took charge of the ID's they had collected, leaving the money in their hands to help defray their expenses. Then he began talking about the situation as the service saw it,

"Isobel is the name for extremely elusive agent/spy/assassin that apparently operates internationally. He or she has no political affiliation as far as we are aware, probably working both sides of the political line equally. It appears that money is the only motivation. Isobel is credited with several killings, at least two kidnaps, and possibly one huge bank job.

"That's it. However we have no real information to go on. I am inclined to suspect that Isobel is a convenient name to hang things onto and has been saddled with crimes she has not committed. However, since you seem to have been targeted, it would really make sense for you to get out of the way in this case."

"Look, JG, we didn't ask for this. If the whole thing came out of your call on us at Boulogne, it implies they are on your tail. Their try at us was clearing the lines, as it were." Abby was sounding a little impatient.

Donny broke in, "I think Abby is right. I am hoping that your car is not bugged. Because if it is, you will have led them straight to our door."

Jonathon stood and went to the door. "You may have a point there. My car should have been swept before I left the Embassy. The same should have applied when I went to Boulogne." He left the RV and walked over to the Peugeot that was parked the other side of the rest area. The small, hand-held sniffer he carried bleeped and flashed as he neared the car.

"Shit!" Jonathon was not happy. He located the bug, a standard signal generator, available anywhere. "Sorry, kids. I seem to have dropped you right in it. Maybe you should reconsider coming in for a while."

"JG, two things. I don't see the attack on us as being part of some international crime syndicate operating in and upon the EU. It had all the marks of a gangland hit. Secondly, I think that bug came from your own people. The one we found was much more sophisticated than yours. I think your boss doesn't really trust you to snag us, and she is taking no chances. So, if you excuse us, we will be getting on our way. Keep in touch."

Donny grabbed Abby and returned to the RV, getting going immediately, pushing the vehicle to get onto the motorway for the last stretch to Paris.

Three days later they made contact with Lotte Joule. They were established in a small hotel on the Avenue de la Republique, in disguise now, with hair dyed and moustache for Donny, the pony-tail wig still in use for the odd occasion. Abby now concentrated on keeping her new hair color and style, with a blond wig for variation when they felt it necessary.

Lotte was a prostitute who worked mainly on the Avenue de la Republique with the odd excursion into the Rue St Denis.

It was on one of these excursions that she met Rabin. Lotte was pretty and twenty-two years old. She was a prostitute from choice, having found that she could not afford the fees to further her college career. She had tried prostitution to gather the funds required as an alternative to asking her parents. She knew they could not afford it.

She decided, after operating for some time with some success, that she enjoyed what she was doing. The returns were well worth the effort.

She was returning from Rue St Denis when she met Rabin. Disliking the look of the man, she had attempted to pass him on the sidewalk. He, of course, had blocked the way. "How much?" He was abrupt, obviously not concerned with the niceties of behavior.

"I'm not interested," she said and attempted to pass.

He reached out and grabbed her arm. She struggled and broke free, trying to run on her high heels. She tripped after a few yards and measured her length on the pavement.

Rabin laughed and caught her as she tried to get up. "Now, come on, girl. I asked how much nicely. So tell me and we can get on with the business."

Lotte looked at the man directly. "I said no! That means no! Now leave me alone and go and find someone else."

She pulled free of his grip and turned to carry on walking.

He raised his hand and slammed her round her face, knocking her against the wall of a house.

"My money is no good then?" He cried, "Then I will take a free sample." He raised his hand to hit her again, and found it would not move. His arm was held firmly. Someone was holding it back. He swung around with a roar of fury, to encounter Donny's fist in his stomach.

Unprepared, he doubled over, meeting Donny's rising knee. At that point things got rather confused and Rabin collapsed to the ground. Donny turned to the girl to find that Abby had her arm around her, and was leading her to their hotel just up the street.

"Where do you live?" She said.

Lotte indicated their hotel. "I have an apartment here."

When they went in, the concierge saw Lotte and was concerned. Her face was red where she had been struck by Rabin, and there was blood in her hair where she had struck the wall.

Abby got her key and took Lotte to the small apartment behind the hotel counter. It was one of two; the other was used by the concierge and his mother.

Having seated Lotte, Abby took water and a
cloth and bathed Lotte's head. Donny got ice from
the machine and made a pack for her face.

Lotte was grateful for their help and once she
felt better, she insisted on making coffee for them
both. She explained that she lived here in the hotel.
It was so convenient. "The concierge is friendly. I sit
with his mother in the mornings. It allows him to go
out shopping and see his friends. I pay rent of
course, but much less that the usual."

She was the daughter of a German father and a
French mother. They lived in Strasbourg where they
were both employed as cleaners in the parliament
building. She had come to Paris to study law at the
Sorbonne but found living in Paris too expensive.
One thing led to another. "I guess I just took the easy
way. I knew my parents couldn't afford to fund me,
and I was not able to earn enough waiting on tables
or working at McDonalds.

"I tried prostitution because I quite enjoyed sex.
I had no real interest in anyone, no boyfriends. Nor
was I interested in girls, except as just friends. I suppose 'asexual' says it."

She shrugged her shoulders, a small smile on
her pretty face. "I think I found the career that I was
intended for. I certainly have managed to keep my
account in the black." She giggled. "My mother
would be appalled to hear me say that, but it is true."

Abby said, "Is there anything else we can do for
you?"

"It should be me asking the question. You have done enough for me. Thank you."

As they left, Lotte tapped Donny on the shoulder and, with an impish smile, whispered, "If you feel like a little light relief, it will be on the house." She smiled as she said it but her eyes were serious.

Donny blushed, and beat a hasty retreat.

The concierge was not a criminal, nor was he vindictive normally. But he did have a soft spot for Lotte. He picked up the telephone when the others were all out of hearing and dialled a local number. When it was answered he spoke, "Rabin attacked my good friend, Lotte, who lives here at the hotel. Please ask him to keep his hands to himself and tell him not to bother my friend." He smiled when he put the phone down, confident that Rabin would behave himself in future.

The following morning, Donny asked the concierge if he had heard of 'Isobel' among his acquaintances in the shadow world of the city.

When they came in from a visit to the Louvre, it was the early evening that same day. They found the concierge in a state of some concern.

"This person, Isobel. I have asked a friend. He said it is dangerous to speak the name. It is rumoured that this Isobel is a contract killer, among other things. Though my friend says that he thinks, perhaps, Isobel is credited with things, he or she could not possibly do."

"You say he or she. Is Isobel not a woman?"

He shrugged, both hands raised; expressing to the world the complete lack of knowledge by a Frenchman. "Who knows? Some say one thing. Others say another." Shaking his head he returned to his place at the desk.

The apartment overlooking the river was the top floor of one of those tall terraces of buildings facing the river. The cathedral of Notre Dame stood on the Isle de Cite almost facing the large window of the apartment. From the window, Isobel could watch the passing scene on the river. Normally this would have a soothing effect. The sight of the seemingly endless parade, moving in both directions along the waterway, reminding her that life goes on regardless of the petty problems of the people it carries and passes.

She turned away and walked over to her computer, a laptop sitting waiting on her desk. Isobel Cartier was in her thirties. She had been married. Her husband, an engineer with Standard Oil, had worked in the Middle East. They had two daughters. After their first year living in caravans in various unpleasant places, Charles, her husband had settled her in this apartment, a permanent home, to bring up the family they started the same year. They were happy, despite the regular absences made necessary by Charles's work. Her second daughter was born and life improved. Charles's reputation grew, and the demand for his expertise commanded higher fees.

Her mind went back to when the family had been on holiday, sailing in the Red Sea. Little Claudette—her youngest—had been three years old, bulged out by her lifejacket and bouncing with her sister on the stretched canvas of the dinghy which stood on chocks between the masts of the big ketch.

The dhow had been just one of the craft like many others to be seen in the region. It was motoring fairly swiftly south toward the Indian Ocean. Isobel had gone below to get cold drinks for everyone. Charles was watching the girls. The self-steering was keeping the boat pretty much on course.

While Isobel was below she heard the chatter of automatic gunfire. She poked her head out of the cabin in time to see both girls blasted in a welter of blood over the side of the ketch. Charles managed one cry, "Nooo......" before he collapsed on deck, dead. The automatic shotgun was loaded and clipped to the bulkhead beside her. She didn't think about it. It was a nightmare. Her family was dead, no warning, no mercy, gone. The dhow came alongside. In cold outrage she waited on the cabin step, shotgun cocked and ready.

Four men stood laughing waiting to board. She shot four times bracing the gun against her hip. All four men died on the spot. A fifth man and a woman ran out of the wheelhouse, guns ready. Isobel swung the gun and shot them both offhand. She reloaded the gun and, making sure the dhow was securely tied on, climbed aboard, avoiding the dead people lying on the deck. She searched the boat, finding three other people, a man with his wife and daughter, locked in the forward cabin. It seemed they had purchased passage to Dar es Salaam. As soon as the boat had sailed from Suez they had been locked in. They had been fed and allowed to clean themselves, but they had already been promised a future as slaves. They confirmed that there were no others aboard.

Isobel asked the man if he would care to take the dhow for himself. 'Spoils of war', as she put it. He declined gracefully but firmly. He considered that the boat would be known along the coast, and the pirates would have friends. So they decided it would be best destroyed.

Sharks had already gathered attracted by the blood in the water. So, having searched the pockets of the dead pirates, all were pushed over the side. The sharks went mad.

Isobel could do nothing about her daughters. But she could not just ditch Charles along with the pirates.

The woman and her daughter helped her wrap Charles's body in cloth found in the dhow, and taking the weapons of the pirates, their money, and a supply of extra food, they cast the dhow adrift, with Charles's body laid on the cabin roof.

As the ketch drew away, the first flicker of flame appeared faint in the sunlight. The smoke rose in the air as the wind took hold of the fire and drove it into a raging inferno. The fuel tanks exploded with a dull whump. The dhow was soon reduced to a skeleton that, weighed by the massive diesel engine, disappeared hissing beneath the waves.

The legend of Isobel had started on the voyage to Dar es Salaam. A pirate boat from Somalia had decided to take the ketch and her owners for ransom.

Using a grenade launcher taken from the dhow, Isobel waited until the pirate's rib-raider was in range, then she deliberately fired three grenades into the boat, reducing the pirates and their boat to ashes. Her passengers were impressed.

She dropped them in Dar es Salaam and sold the boat. The weapons also found a ready market. She returned to Paris by air. The story of the ruthless slaughter of the pirates spread along the coast, becoming part of the legend of the area.

With recognition, the name 'Isobel' started acquiring a reputation based on rumour. It seemed that whenever anything occurred with no simple explanation, they blamed Isobel. Just a name to most people, but as a result, contracts were put out on her. Criminals were persuaded that she had been responsible for some interference with their affairs.

Her return to Paris seemed like an invitation to every independent killer in France to collect a little easy money.

They reckoned without the sheer strength of character that was concealed under the mild exterior of the attractive lady. Instincts developed during the past few weeks prepared her to react when the first attempt on her life was made. Her experience on the ketch had been traumatic, but she had been forced to learn how to survive.

Two men, complete with proper identification, had called to check the electricity. They might have succeeded if they had done their homework properly. They should have chosen another option. The electricity had been checked three days before.

She had been loath to react when she discovered the list in the pocket of one of her would be assassins. The names had meant little until she came across Jonathon Glynn's name linked to two others, a man and a woman, Donny Weston and Abby Marshall.

Jonathon was in the office in the Embassy when the call came asking for him by name.

He pressed the record button from habit and lifted the receiver.

"Glynn here. Can I help you?"

"I rang to let you know that you and your two friends have been listed. Contracts have been issued on all three of you. The origin seems to be Mob, possibly Chinese. Your friends have dropped out of sight, but you are very high profile at present. Be warned,"

"Who are you?" Jonathon asked quickly, before the phone was put down.

"I'm Isobel." The voice said, followed by the click ending the call.

"Well," mused Jonathon aloud. "It seems that Isobel is female at least."

He called Donny on the secure phone. Getting no answer he left a message, advising them that Isobel was a woman and that she had given him a warning that they were on the contract list with him.

Abby rang back later. "Thanks, JG. We got the message. Remember the three Chinese in the Camargue." She left it at that.

"You're both alright?"

"Yes. We're fine and not too far away actually."

"I was warned by a woman calling herself Isobel. Although I cannot be sure, I think people may have the wrong impression about her. Anyway, I think it safe to assume that we are all three still under threat. So keep an eye over your shoulder at all times.

David O'Neil

Chapter Three

Lotte sat chatting with Abby in the lobby of the hotel. The street door opened. Neither girl seemed to notice the man who strode in. For several seconds he stood waiting for attention. Then he rang the bell for the concierge. When he rang the second time, Abby looked up. As if she had just spotted him, she said "The concierge will be back in a moment."

"The visitor smiled, "You are English? Perhaps you can help. I am looking for an English girl, blond. Her name is Abby Marshall. I understand she is staying here."

Abby shrugged, "As far as I know there is no one of that name here, but I will enquire when the concierge returns. Who shall I say is looking for her?"

"I am from the British Embassy." He produced a card with the embassy crest on it, stating that he was Arthur Creech-Jones, passport office.

"Can I ask what you want with her, Mr Creech-Jones?" Abby asked in English.

"You may not, young lady. That is between Miss Marshall and me." He sounded a little abrupt, not used to being questioned that was for sure.

"Then, Mr Creech-Jones, I shall not bother trying to locate her. Paris is notorious for the white slave trade. I do not know you nor am I reassured by your manner. Why, you could be anyone, not even from the Embassy. I have never seen you there." Since the only occasion she had visited the embassy had been with Jonathon and entry via the back door, it was not surprising that Abby did not recognize the man.

"I came with a message from a Mr. Jonathon Glynn. You may tell Miss Marshall." The man turned to go.

"Ah, Mr. Jones. Perhaps you could give me the message from Mr Glynn. I will pass it on."

"So, you do know Miss Marshall. Well, just tell her I called and the name is Creech-Jones." Once more he set out for the door.

"Oh, Mr. Creech-Jones. Please pass your message. I am in fact Miss Marshall, Abby Marshall. What did Jonathon say?"

Creech-Jones looked accusingly at Abby. "Why did you not say so in the first place? You are not blond anyway. How do I know you are who you say you are?"

"Because I am aware that Jonathon Glynn has an unadvertised post at the Embassy. The message must be of important otherwise you would not be carrying it."

Mr Creech-Jones turned red. He thrust a letter at Abby and stalked out. Abby caught him on the step.

"I am sorry, sir. I am being hunted by some very nasty people and have to be extremely careful. Jonathon at the Embassy is a friend of the family and has been keeping an eye on things for me." She said nothing of Donny, making sure to give as little away as possible since Mr Creech-Jones failed to mention Donny either. After an anxious moment, Abby remembered '*the need to know*'.

Mollified, Arthur Creech-Jones, the man from the Embassy, departed on his next errand.

Isobel Cartier looked around the apartment with regret. Her bags were packed and the car was outside the delivery door of the block. There were many happy memories associated with this place, and she would miss the view across the river below. The stall-holders had become familiar over the years she had lived here. She straightened her shoulders and started the dumb waiter, carrying the bags to the ground floor. Turning and descending the four flights of stairs with practiced ease, she arrived before the old lift had creaked to a halt.

She looked at the two bags which contained all she was taking with her. Not a lot to show for so many happy years, but maybe too much for the life-style she had been driven to adopt.

With a shrug, she lifted the bags and carried them out to the parked Peugeot.

Quite openly, she loaded the last bag into the cavernous trunk of the car, and turned and looked back at the building that had been her home for so long.

Then, without further delay, she climbed into the driver's seat and drove off.

The watcher made a call on his cell phone. He received his instructions and left the rented room, bag in hand, his part of the job done.

Meanwhile Isobel drove to the car park at Charles de Gaulle airport. In the multi-story section she left the car and took the walkway to the terminal. Her transition into a dowdy, elderly cleaner was accomplished after she entered a private lounge. Her shadow watched her enter. Later he saw her leave the lounge to board a private jet parked on the stand opposite the field side of the lounge.

The cleaner, unnoticed, mopped her way to the main concourse where she followed another staff member through the private door to the staff side of the busy terminal.

The smartly-uniformed flight attendant passed the watcher, trailing her wheeled bag behind her. Apart from noticing the elegant rear view of the blue-skirted young woman, the watcher was unaware that his quarry had just eluded him, for the second time.

The hire car was where she had left it. Isobel drove to her apartment building and parked in the service area at the rear. Her distinctive uniform hat was no longer to be seen, the uniform jacket was now deposited in the wheeled bag.

The dark wig still in place, she got out of the car and stepped down a short flight of stairs to the basement apartment of her building. She punched in the door code and entered the two bed-roomed flat.

Standing the wheeled bag beside the hall closet, she went into the lounge and sat back on the settee with a tired sigh.

The whole building had been purchased when she and Charles had first chosen the place. Her father had bought it through a corporation for tax purposes. They had converted the building into a series of apartments. Though on paper she still paid rent, in fact she was reimbursed though the trust that maintained the building. The basement flat had become vacant when she and Charles were cruising. Because of all the turmoil at the time of the attempted hi-jack, the flat had not been re-let. By then she had realized that she may need a bolt-hole, a place to hide. The basement apartment was ideal. It was just a question of keeping it anonymous.

Isobel had removed all her personal things to the basement over the past two days, having reasoned that the opposition would continue to hound her. Hopefully the elaborate charade of earlier today would have bought not only time but anonymity for a while at least.

Abby lifted her glass and sipped the cool wine. The two were sitting, waiting for Jonathon to appear at the café mentioned in his message. Donny spotted him along the street coming in their direction "Here he comes at last," he said to Abby. Puzzled, he saw Jonathon dart into a side road ahead.

Taking Abby's hand, Donny dropped money on the table for the bill. Leaving the table, he casually wandered down the road, Abby beside him, leaning on his shoulder like young lovers everywhere.

Both, under their casual exterior, were alert for any sign of the reason for Jonathon's hasty change of direction.

There were two of them: standing, reading their newspapers rather too casually. Both were dressed in dark blue suits described by Abby as Shanghai shabby. Neither looked particularly comfortable. Shoulders tense, the taller man shooting glances across the road.

The third man was seated in front of an ignored pot of coffee and a croissant at the cafe opposite. His attention was fixed on the approaching stream of people, searching back and forth. Not obviously looking for somebody, but to Abby's eye definitely searching.

Donny turned and smiled at her, brushing her ear with his lips, "Jonathon is with us," he breathed. They turned into '*Bon Marche*' the department store, still wandering, idly scanning the window display before strolling in. Jonathon walked briskly past them as they heard the automatic doors sigh shut behind them. Inside they followed the now sauntering, figure of their friend through the various departments to the side entrance. Out of sight of the watchers they all piled into a cab.

Later, in the privacy of the Embassy office, the three friends discussed the current state of affairs.

Both Abby and Donny were well aware of the experience and skill of their mentor. Jonathon in turn had no doubts about the growing expertise in the two young people before him. His main preoccupation was to ensure that they did not over-step the line between their growing skills and their enthusiasm to remove the threat to themselves and their friends.

Jonathon's position as passport officer at the Embassy did require his presence at some of the official functions that were so much part of the diplomatic scene.

The Summer Ball was one of the many attended by the diplomatic glitterati of all nations, present in the Paris scene. Jonathon was required to attend. "I think it might be an advantage if you two attend in your own shape and form. It will be noticed and should enhance the effect of your altered appearance in disguise. You could manage the transformation for one night. I'll book a room at, perhaps, the George V hotel for the occasion. The formal dress 'do' might well produce the appearance of whoever it is that is pursuing you. I cannot rid myself of the feeling that the Chinese Embassy is the base for their current operation, legal or otherwise. What do you think?"

Abby's eyes lit up at the thought of attending a formal ball but, sensible girl that she was, she didn't immediately jump in with both feet.

"That could be a good way of bringing the mice out of the woodwork," she said casually. "I noticed a ball gown in *Nouvelles Galeries* that should be suitable, if you think the budget will run to it?" Her raised eyebrow was directed at Donny.

He nodded, "Yes, I think that would be good idea, and I think our Chinese friends have donated enough to cover the costs." He referred to the money gleaned from their various attackers over the past weeks.

Jonathon interjected, "I think I can outfit you, Donny. I will be in dress uniform for the occasion. Carol will partner me, and you two will be my guests." The matter decided he went on to caution them. "It seems that there are not only the Chinese involved. I have heard whispers that the Harry Sanders group have been replaced by a rather grotesque character known as *le Grenouille (the Frog)*, but only behind his back. His real name is Marak, Pierre Marak; Algerian. He suffers from glaucoma and has protruding eyes and a receding chin, a most unfortunate combination that has earned him his nickname. He knows of it but hates it and has been known to seriously disfigure anyone he hears using it. His operation works from Rue St Denis, and so far, covers the usual areas of prostitution, extortion, robbery, murder etc.

The ball was a sparkling affair, the variety of colorful uniforms set off by the equally colorful dresses of the ladies. Abby looked stunning in her royal blue gown, her blond hair and fair complexion combining to make her stand out in the glittering throng.

Donny, dressed in dinner jacket with black tie, had also made the effort. His equally blond, clean-cut looks had attracted many an interested eye among the ladies present.

Jonathon Glynn, resplendent in Rifle-Regiment Green with gold facings, joined them accompanied by a radiant Carol Varenne in a close-fitting, gold gown, displaying discreetly the triple diamond engagement ring received from Jonathon that very evening. The four friends were soon ensconced at a table set back from the edge of the dance floor, already alive with couples rotating to the rhythm of a waltz. The congratulations over, the four started to take note of the other people present.

The Chinese visitors were not as easy to pick out as Abby had imagined. Several of the other South-East Asian countries were represented by people of Chinese descent. The services of Jonathon's skilled eye were needed as he managed to identify by name several of the individuals present.

The senior so-called cultural attaché was a smooth-faced man of slender build. His bland face concealed a very smart mind, according to Jonathon. There were several others, pointed out by Jonathon, with dubious credentials. Carol was quick to remind them that Jonathon himself had no room to talk. His own credentials, including the uniform he was wearing, were part of his cover. His own uniform would have been an obvious giveaway as he was still part of the Intelligence Corps.

While they danced and chatted there were several encounters with other guests. The Chinese attaché pointed out by Jonathon came and spoke with the two women, complimenting them both on their appearance.

They had been introduced by one of the other Embassy staff who seemed to spend his entire evening introducing people to each other in a seemingly random manner. Jonathon later confirmed that the pattern of introductions was planned and the apparent random nature of the performance was obtained by the natural scattering of the assembled guests requiring ingenuity to bring them successfully together.

Donny had observed the meeting between the Chinese, Wu Fat, and Abby. The slight hesitation when he had realised that Abby was the subject of a kill order would have been unnoticed by an idle watcher. He had noticed because he was looking specifically for reaction.

Discussing the matter with the others the following day, he gave his opinion that the Chinese had been unaware of the people nominated for execution, thus far just names. Meeting Abby was probably a shock. "Do you think we are dealing with a rogue outfit within the Chinese ranks, perhaps a Chinese version of CIA?"

"Are you implying that the CIA has rogue elements? Tsk, tsk. Why on earth would you think that?" Jonathon said drily.

"That is beside the point. Am I right?"

"Partially! In China there are the usual divisions between the major movers in the Government. These differences are reflected down the line and very often expanded, the lower down you get. As things are, I believe our friend Mr Wu Fat is rightly concerned about the group of so-called agents wandering around Europe targeting a selection of people on the basis of passing acquaintance with the intelligence world.

"He will undoubtedly be aware that when or rather if the cat gets out of the bag, he will be in direct line of fire from above. This, only because he is technically, director of covert operations for the European Union, and regardless of whether he has or has not been made aware of the presence of a cowboy outfit working in his backyard."

Sitting back, Jonathon allowed himself a sip of his drink.

Both of the men standing in front of Pierre Marak were uncomfortable, shifting from foot to foot, neither would meet his eye.

"So you decided to let the slant-eyed bunch get on with what they were doing?"

The taller of the two nodded," It seemed the easiest thing to do; they were all tooled up with shooters, and there were three of them."

"So what went wrong? They were dealing with a couple of kids. What happened?"

Hesitantly the tall man said, "They thought it would be a pushover and they found they were dealing with a pair of gunslingers. Both kids hit the ditches with guns up and shooting before the Chinese realized. The first went down dead. The second was wounded, and hit the dirt bleeding like a stuck pig. The third sprayed bullets everywhere, hitting nothing. He jumped up and I swear that bitch plugged him twice in the chest." He stopped, looking apprehensively at his boss. Then continued; "The bleeder bled out on the roadside. We watched through binoculars, we were too far away to interfere. By the time we reached the place the kids had gone."

Marak stroked his receding chin reflectively. He made no comment on the fact that his two men had made no effort to finish off what the Chinese had started. Their brief had after all been to find out what the Chinese were up to, then dispose of them.

"Find out who the kids are and why the Chinese were after them."

"Should we ice them, boss?"

"You heard what I said. Just do what you're told."

The two men hastily left the room, relieved that they had survived.

Marak turned to man standing behind him. "When they come back with the information, drop them into the foundations somewhere. They are idiots. I can live without them working for me."

Peter Carver nodded, "Do we have any idea what the Chinese are up to?"

Had anyone else asked the question Marak might easily shot him. As Marak's number two, he occupied a privileged position. At six-foot three, the big Russian had been on the run from his Mafia bosses when the two men chasing him had cornered him. He had more or less resigned himself to the death he had been promised. The Citroen had come around the corner and smashed into the two hit-men before crashing into the building behind them. Marak had walked round the corner after the car and looked at the carnage, two dead in the car, and two against the wall. When he spotted Peter he lifted the gun in his right hand, only to stop as he observed Peter's, already lined up on his chest.

Peter had spoken quietly, "I do not wish to shoot you. You have just saved my life, so shall we depart this scene before the Gendarmerie appear and spoil the conversation we will undoubtedly have."

Marak hesitated for a second only. Then he put the gun away and jerked his head for Peter to follow him, and that was that. The Russian had slotted into Marak's organisation and almost immediately became a vital part of the group. He had swiftly risen to his present position, partially because he was the only person with the nerve to tell Marak the truth.

Because of that, and because he was efficient at his work. Marak had realised that life was much easier with him around.

Isobel Cartier was bored. She had been settled into the basement apartment for nearly two days and already she was missing the view over the river. Sitting and thinking about her situation she realized that, although she had plenty of money and places to live, there was a villa in Antibes, and in addition to this house, her parent's house in Guildford in Surrey, just south of London. It was currently rented by an American actor starring in a 'West End Show'.

Enough was enough. She got to her feet and stalked into her bedroom. Removing the dark wig from its stand, she swiftly donned it, making sure her naturally fair hair was totally covered. Then, adding touches of darker make-up she toned down her cheeks, giving her face a more drawn appearance. The Hermes scarf, went well with her casual jacket, and denim skirt. Donning suede boots, she was ready to issue forth into the cool spring day.

She felt better the moment she stepped out of the door, though habit dictated that she carefully scan the area as she climbed the steps to the street from the basement apartment.

Seeing nothing unusual, she strode off towards the river and the art display that was always on view there.

She spied the two Chinese walking slowly along the river bank studying everyone they encountered intently. She immediately thought of Jonathon Glynn and his two young friends. It did not occur to her that they may be looking for her. As she passed them she caught a glimpse of one taking a second look at her. Then she heard the voice call out, "Is-o-bel."

It took all her self control to stop herself turning at the sound of the call, but she managed and when eventually she was able to look behind her, the two Chinese were gone.

Why me? She thought. *Why should they want me, for Pete's sake?*

Chapter Four

Under pressure from Donny and Abby, Jonathon was explaining why he thought the couple were under threat from the Chinese. "I have been involved with the release of several Chinese dissidents. This has made me a target. Since I am apparently a member of the Embassy I am to some extent protected. But all the people I have been in contact with are at risk. The targeting of you two has come about because of the episode of the dispersal of Harry Sanders and his gang. It seems word has got about of your part in things. By visiting you I am afraid I have placed your lives in danger. I seriously suggest that you get back onto the boat and sail off to distant parts, for your own sake and for my peace of mind."

"And who will watch your back?" Abby sounded impatient. "I have not seen any sign of backup. In fact, apart from the warning given by 'Isobel', I have seen no attempt by your department to interfere with the actions of this Chinese Mob."

Donny spoke for the first time on the subject. "What you have not told us is who our attackers are.

I know they are Chinese and I understand there is some connection to the Embassy. I suspect that they are not Chinese government agents at all. The whole business so far smells of private enterprise. What about it?"

"I think you may be right; one of the problems is that the dissidents being released are on some occasions in possession of valuable information both economic and intrinsic. In addition, I am now informed that the local villains are showing an interest." He held up his hand to stop them "Nothing overt yet but they do seem to be appearing on the fringes. That means trouble."

"So what you are saying is that internal matters in China are being masterminded from here? You are involved presumably to keep matters discreet. Chinese hit-men have been brought here to back up the team blocking the efforts of your lot?" He looked at Jonathon with a raised eyebrow. When Jonathon nodded, he continued, "Just to confuse matters completely, we now have another bunch of freelance entrepreneurs joining the queue who probably have no idea of what the others are doing. They just smell profit. Does that cover it?"

"Just about. Officially the Embassies, Chinese and ours, know nothing about this. Everything has been kept under the counter and that is the way we wish to keep it."

Abby looked at Donny. "Time for us to leave the field to the experts, don't you think? It's one thing to get involved when we know who and why we are fighting, but I'm not too happy about being dragged in as a diversion. I refuse to be cannon fodder for the sake of some Chinese jailbird."

"The trouble as I see it is that we are already targets and the boat is known. I vote we wring the information we require out of our good friend here. Then at least we can make an informed choice whether we are better off staying or going." With that Donny turned on Jonathon who was starting to get up from his chair, and rammed him back into the seat.

"You dropped us into this situation, now explain!"

Jonathon looked at Donny and saw from the look in his eye that he was not in the mood for being given the run-around.

"Very well, I did my best to keep you clear of this. On your own heads be it." For the next ten minutes he spoke without interruption.

When he finished, Abby said, "And that's it, the whole thing?"

"It is, and the plates are stashed here in France where the paper is available, as is the printing expertise. The three men will arrive during the next two days. But we only know their rendezvous. We don't know the time or which of the prisoners are involved. We do suspect that one man, known as John Ling, is one of the three."

"Why France? With all the resources China has, why come to France to forge Chinese money?"

"Chinese, did I say Chinese money? It's not Chinese money. It's U.S. dollars, fifty and one hundred dollar bills."

"But surely then, this is a matter for the U.S. Treasury?" Abby was confused.

"They are not aware of this. Bluntly, neither the French nor the Chinese want U.S. agents here in France to add to the confusion we are already experiencing. They will be told when we have wrapped things up."

"What is all this to do with us? Are we just a diversion? And what about Isobel? Why is she involved?"

"Your involvement is strictly by chance, as is Isobel's, from what I can see. I think we have a clash of interests between the Chinese and the local mob. To sum up, I think – only think, mind you – that the local mob sniffed out the Chinese interest and, without knowing what or why, they stepped in. I think they were shadowing the gunmen that tried to take you two out in the Camargue. Seeing what happened, you became of interest, especially when they saw the way you dealt with your attackers. Isobel has, I believe, been credited with all sorts of things that she has had nothing to do with. I am sure that the story of her troubles in the Red Sea and beyond are fairly accurate. But for the rest I think she has been a convenient target to shoot at. Blame for incidents she could not have been involved in has been attributed to her. She is therefore, a target, with a price on her head."

"She must be feeling very lonely and vulnerable with nobody to cover her back and all sort of villainy being carried out in her name." Abby sounded concerned. "Would it not be a good idea to bring her in with us? It would increase our own security and hers at the same time. It would also make our job of sorting this out easier."

Donny looked at her with admiration and pride. "That's my girl, a sniff of gun smoke and she is off on the trail. So how can we contact Isobel?"

Jonathon said sardonically, "The simple answer is we cannot. We have no idea where she is."

"She phoned you, Jonathon. You automatically trace all calls you receive. At least you will have a number."

Jonathon shrugged. He told himself that he had tried to keep them out of this affair. It seemed though, that they were a magnet for trouble. From his pocket he took a small notebook. He opened it and read out a series of numbers.

Abby input the information.

"Hullo?" The voice was female and sounded soft and cultured. "Hullo, who is this?"

"Isobel?" The line went quiet, then, "Who is this?"

"My name is Abby. My friend, Donny, and I are friends of Jonathan Glynn." She stopped and waited.

"This is Isobel. What is it you want?"

"Can we meet? I think we have a common interest. We will be happy to see you at a place of your choosing, and as soon as possible. We have had a few narrow escapes and I understand you also have had problems." She paused, waiting.

"The Orangery, in thirty minutes. You two and Glynn. No others, understand?"

"We will be there." She put the phone down. "The Orangery, thirty minutes. Let's go."

The Monet wall panels had never really excited Donny. He did enjoy the work of many of the other impressionists and some of Monet's other work. But the endless lily ponds of the exhibition in the Orangery did nothing for him.

The voice behind him took him by surprise. "You must be Donny, Abby's friend."

He swung slowly around, looking at the paintings as if following the panels around in sequence. He finally faced Isobel. He smiled, an instant reaction to the attractive lady standing in front of him. He took her outstretched hand. "You have to be Isobel. I was told you were beautiful. It was certainly no exaggeration." He bent and lightly kissed her hand.

Isobel blushed. "I was told you were a young man. I did not expect such politesse. You flatter me.

I was looking for Abby, and also the redoubtable Jonathon."

"This way, madam. They are through the archway." He took her arm and they walked together toward the arched entrance to the other half of the exhibition. As they approached they heard a voice.

"Just keep your hands in view, both of you. Where is the other one, I was told there were three of you. Mic, take a look through there." They heard the approaching footsteps of Mic. There was nowhere to hide. Donny drew his gun, pointed it and placing his finger to his lips, faced the archway. Isobel stepped off to the side instinctively drawing her own pistol from her handbag.

Mic came though the arch almost trotting. He saw Donny's gun pointing at his face, and the other in the hand of the lady. He also saw in time, the finger to Donny's lips and kept his mouth shut.

The rough voice from the other room shouted, "Hurry up. Is he there?"

Donny indicated the entrance. Mic got the message. "He is probably outside. I'll check."

Donny nodded and held his hand out. Mic gave him his gun. Isobel spun the man round and frisked him, producing a flick knife. Donny unloaded Mic's gun and returned it to him. He whispered to Isobel, so that Mic could hear. "I'm his prisoner, you stay right behind him with the knife. If he twitches, kill him." He turned to Mic. "Meet Isobel!"

Mic blanched. Her reputation had gone before her. "Okay, I got the message."

"Tell your friend you've found me and are bringing me in."

"I've got him, Max. That makes all three."

"Good work." The speaker was standing with his gun on Abby and Jonathon. Both had their hands up. On the floor were their two automatics. Donny led the way with his hand behind him, as if he was being held by Mic, who had a visible gun in his hand. Isobel was hidden by the two men in front of her.

Things happened fast. Donny dropped to the floor, as the man looked at the newcomers. Abby and Jonathon dropped at the same time. Donny's gun was up and he fired while the gunman was still making his mind up. Donny's shot hit the man in the chest.

The shot in reply hit Mic in the shoulder. He swore, "Stupid bastard. Thought he was John Wayne." He staggered and would have fallen had not Isobel caught him.

"Out, quick. We were lucky the place is empty. Let's get out before someone comes."

Abby swiftly took the dead man's wallet and emptied his other pockets, stuffing the whole lot in her handbag. As they left the Orangery they noticed the sign outside placed by their ambushers. It stated that the exhibition was being renewed so the building was closed for the day.

The Hotel in the Avenue de la Republic was quiet. The concierge sensibly made himself scarce as soon as he provided the medical kit. Isobel and Abby between them soon had Mic bandaged up, and if not comfortable, certainly feeling better with a cognac in his hand.

He sang like a canary. He knew Marak would not forgive him so his only hope was to get out of Paris. Perhaps back to his home territory in Agen. The pity was he knew nothing, except of course, the identity of the boss and his deputy, Peter Carver, the Russian.

He had no idea why they had been told to capture Donny and Abby. They had been spotted by chance on their way to the Orangery that morning. While they chatted before going in, the two gunmen had entered, then tied up the attendant on duty and found the sign. Mic had stepped outside as the others went in. Putting the sign in place, he raced round to the exit and entered that way.

Max, Mic's partner/boss, was always rash and they were in trouble because of his rashness already. That was why he jumped the gun with Jonathon and Abby. "See how far that got him." Mic was unsympathetic about his partner. "He asked for it, after all."

They gave Mic the money from his partner's wallet, and saw him off on the train to Agen. It was the last they saw or heard of him.

They were then able to sit down with Isobel and discuss the situation. As Abby suggested the idea of joining forces appealed to her, and they agreed to use the hotel as their base of operations.

The silence in the office of Pierre Marak was not a peaceful calm reflection of the atmosphere of tranquillity that could have been found there. It was rather the calm that comes before the storm. Marak sat at his desk reading a note he had found when he came in that morning. The few words had excited Marak. He now knew what was causing the Chinese to panic: printing plates for U.S. dollars, a licence to print money. The note suggested that there was a clue to the location of the plates. The best way to find them was to find the man who was coming to use them. John Ling.

Obviously the man would not be arriving in Paris on a scheduled airline. It was likely he would be travelling on the underground route, via container ship or tramp steamer.

Among the members of the criminal fraternity there are certain things that are general knowledge. One of those things is the smuggling route. There are several different versions of this, some more favoured than others. While it would have been difficult to cover all routes (the manpower would have been considerable), there were certain favoured routes that were feasible. At present there were three, all as yet undiscovered by the law. One of these was linked with short sea routes only. The other two were part of the Seven Seas routes and were probably a more likely prospect for the interception of the traveller from China.

Chapter Five

Marak called Peter in. "Put watchers on the underground from China. I wish to interview anyone who comes in unaccompanied, or with just one companion. Start now!"

"Yes, boss." Peter did not argue.

John Ling was not happy. He was cold and uncomfortable. The container he was travelling in had condensation running down the walls. The other people travelling together with him were all huddled up around him trying to keep warm and dry.

He realized he had been conned by the agent who had arranged his escape from Shanghai. Revenge would be sweet once he got out of this container. His contact in France was supposed to have money and new papers. All he had to do was to get there. Le Havre was an easy train journey to Paris where his contact was established. He shivered and cuddled up to his neighbour, a young Chinese girl with a realistic view on life. He felt her fingers fumbling to undo the clothing between them and he moved back to let her slip the material still between them out of the way. At first her skin felt cold, but gradually the contact of their bare skin combined to give a feeling of warmth. She adjusted their clothing to cover their bodies completely, sliding beneath him, spreading herself to receive him. He was grateful for feeling needed and the warmth they produced between them.

Ignoring the other people around them, the couple moved minimally, the sex secondary to the warmth they were generating.

Of the other twelve people in the container, they knew nothing and cared less. Two were already dead, victims of hypothermia. Three others were rapidly reaching that state. The activity of John Ling and the girl aroused little interest, and past the stage of shivering, the three died later that night.

When their prison was opened the following day, the dead were tossed overboard. The survivors were fed hot food and their clothing washed and dried off. This was not an act of kindness. It was purely pragmatic. The container was hosed out and the rubbish from the five-week journey also dumped. The box was moved into a slot between two others by the ship's own crane while, from a second, several pallets of electronic equipment were moved in, to give the appearance of a full load. Blankets and food were placed in the far end and as the coast of France drew nearer, the seven surviving immigrants were ushered in and the last pallet inserted, closing them off once more. With doors closed and sealed, another container was shifted back to block off the smuggled passenger's cell.

The watchers nearly missed the group of people leaving the docks. John Ling was lucky. The young Chinese girl was still with him. Together they had split from the others as soon as they had been released.

He was no fool. He was well aware that the people who had arranged his escape from Shanghai, would want to keep him under observation. To them it was a commercial operation. In their business the girl, now she had arrived, would normally be already on her way to a brothel to work off an invented debt. He would be passed to either a slave trader or perhaps to agents of his political enemies, of which there were many. It was one of the reasons he had kept the girl with him. If only one person was expected, the slightest alteration of circumstances could be to his advantage.

The other factor was that he suspected she was working for his benefactors. She had come to him just a little too easily. Too willing for the daughter of wealthy, former diplomats. She was supposed to be escaping to join her dissident parents in Paris. Their fortune had been discreetly stashed away in Europe before her parents ran. Her story was that she was meant to go with them but had been delayed at the last minute, so had to travel alone.

Expecting one person, Marak's men gathered the group together and learned that five had died en-route. The five survivors did not know who John ling was. They did know who he wasn't. They suggested he must be the other man who had spent time having sex with the girl.

They shrugged when they were asked where the couple had gone.

The appearance of two Gendarmes at the street corner closed that line of enquiry. The group and their interrogators split up, departing the vicinity with haste.

John Ling was tall for a Chinese; nearly six foot, he was slim and fit. His internment had literally been house arrest. He had overcome the privations of his initial prison sentence with exercise and by continuing his practice of Tae-kwon-do, a discipline he had kept up whenever he was permitted in prison. He spoke French and English fluently, and could pass for a local of either country. His companion, Mary Tang, was from Hong Kong. Brought up in the 'smart set', she was accustomed to getting her own way. The delay in meeting her parents when they left was her own fault. She had sniffed a little too much 'happy dust' and awaken naked in bed with a man she did not recognize. It had happened before. She shrugged, then remembered where she was supposed to be. She still had her watch. Too late, by three hours at least, she had gathered her things together and gone home to the empty house.

Her bag still stood where she had left it, her wallet with her passport and money, credit cards, her life was still there. The tall American was there as well. Axel Morgan was fifty, balding, and he had a proposition.

He took charge of all her things. They would be in France waiting for her to collect them. All she had to do was to travel by the underground route to Europe with a party of others. On the journey she was to contact and attach herself to a man. She had studied the photograph carefully. John Ling was educated and civilized, she was told, and had not enjoyed intimacy for close on five years. The journey would be uncomfortable but not really dangerous. Just five weeks, give or take!

"Listen to what he says and stay with him one way or another all the way to Paris."

She would be protected and followed from the time she left the ship.

As it happened, she found the relationship with John Ling agreeable. He was intelligent, witty and very good company. The time spent in the container had passed in argument and low-key fun. The others in the group had not understood how they could find the situation at all amusing. They had disapproved vehemently.

John was forced to deal with two of the men who became aggressive. He had been quick and efficient, leaving the two men groaning in the arms of their families. Both of the men survived the journey though one lost his wife to pneumonia.

As for John, his relationship with Mary was unexpected and rewarding. Undoubtedly her quick-wittedness and willingness to share her body, and youthful body heat, had helped him to survive. Her presence had also helped when eluding the watchers in France. He found that, though he had planned to dump her as soon as he was clear of Le Havre, when the time came he was reluctant. To his surprise he found he took pleasure from her company.

He finally made up his mind when she confessed that she had been put with the group to keep an eye on him by people she believed were the CIA. He also knew that her parents were wealthy and had settled in Paris.

Mary had been to France before. Her education had included a year at the Sorbonne during which time she had travelled around the country with friends in the VW Camper that was the trademark of the students of the time. She now took over the travel arrangements for the couple and instinctively made sure any watchers would find it almost impossible to keep tabs on them. She was twenty-five years old, and had finally grown up.

Jonathon's people were aware of the arrival of John Ling. They had also noted his companion. The file on Jonathon's desk detailed the chequered career of Mary Tang to date. As he read the litany of drugs and alcohol related offences that signposted her life, he built up a picture of a reckless, spoilt bitch.

He had shown the file to Abby. Her comment was, "If the CIA think she will stay put for their purposes, they are nuts! Take a look. What would you say, Donny?"

Donny studied the file and grinned. "She knew France as a student. They arrive at Le Havre and disappear. She has hooked up with John Ling. I would put money on it. If the CIA expect her to check-in, they are spitting in the wind." He paused for a moment. "My suggestion would be to contact some of her old mates from the Sorbonne. They might be able to suggest where we could look."

Jonathon looked at the two of them. Abby; slim, shapely and athletic, with attractive regular features and an air of confidence. Donny; tall, fair haired and also athletic, with a ready smile.

"You both seen to have made up your minds about this woman."

"She has been existing without direction up to now," Abby said. "Now she has met someone who gives her a purpose, who treats her as a grown-up, ignoring her wealth and beauty, appreciating her common sense and intelligence."

"It's something that happens sometimes," Donny commented, unsurprised at Abby's remarks. "Time to start looking, and we are probably the best suited for that."

Jonathon smiled. He produced a book and handed it to Abby. "This could be of use," he said. Abby looked at it. It was a yearbook for the year that Mary had been in Paris. The students of that time were listed and in many cases photographed. Mary Tang smiled from the page, with a sweet look that belied the list of transgressions produced by Jonathon.

Jonathon said, "You should find one of the crowd she ran around with at that time working as assistant secretary of admissions. I cannot guarantee that they were close but at least it's a starting point."

He turned back to his desk. "Take care out there. The people we are dealing with are dangerous"

Abby and Donny left the office and went into the side room where their alternative rigouts were stored. As they changed their appearances, Donny said, "Why do I get the impression, that the dangerous people Jonathon mentioned are either Chinese or French?"

Abby thought for a moment, "I think the people who sponsored Mary Tang in Hong Kong are not really CIA. They are possibly contractors who have done jobs for them in the past and therefore know the routine. The value of the plates will be astronomic to the right people. The effects on the world economy, of the mass flooding of the market with forged dollars would be crippling. Confidence would evaporate, and trade would cease until some other funding could be introduced. That would mean at present, sterling, euro or yen, or maybe even the Yuan."

"The Yuan?"

"China! That would be an interesting thought, in view of the fact that China is currently one of the richest economies at the moment."

Donny looked at Abby seriously. "Are you thinking what I'm thinking? Why are we discussing plates for U.S. dollars emanating from China? Why were they produced there in the first place? John Tang was not a recognized criminal. He was detained as an intellectual in the first place. He shared prison with artists and artisans. His release followed the disappearance of the plates from China, according to Jonathon."

"And he knows exactly where to find them once again, according to Jonathon."

"I smell rats, big fat rats. I may be mistaken but this feels like a con, someone somewhere is manipulating things. People are being moved around like chessmen." Donny smiled grimly,

"While I would not put it past Jonathon to use us, I draw the line at him putting us in serious danger. He was shocked at the attempt on the boat, and

I think equally shocked at the Camargue incident. From that point on I think we were slipped into the pattern as a couple of reserve pieces. What do you think?"

"I'm inclined to agree. Let's take a look at this so-called contact at the Sorbonne and take it from there."

They crossed the river at the Ile de la Cite, following the Rue Saint Jacques to the University. Parking the hired car, they ambled into the area, mixing easily with the student population present at most times of the day in the area.

Inside the building the signs indicated the location of the admissions office and there they ran their quarry to earth.

Marcel Albert was mid-twenties and running to fat. His receding hairline had been disguised to some extent by the careful arrangement of his remaining locks that rather curiously framed his semi-shaven cheeks. The petulant look he adopted did nothing to hide his frustration at having to deal with a succession of trivial matters, when he had obviously been destined for greater things. In the yearbook he had expected to become snapped up by at least one of the major political parties, to be groomed for high office.

The glitch in his career arrangements had caused him to become bitter and envious of his luckier colleagues.

Thus the request by Donny and Abby gave him a rare opportunity to vent his bitterness on an object of envy from his past. Mary Tang had everything: daughter of a millionaire, breezed through her education without apparent effort, and spurned the approaches of lowly, hard-working students like himself.

"Such information is not available to visitors!"

"I did not ask for official information." Donny was inclined to be short with the man whom he instinctively disliked.

Abby stepped in smiling. "We are students at Oxford, and we were considering coming to the Sorbonne for an interim year in our courses. I was given the name of Mary Tang as a contact who might put us in the picture, you know, the current scene over here." She dropped her eyes hesitantly. "I was also told that you were the person to ask, since you, defacto, run the secretariat here."

Donny stared in admiration at his partner, half persuaded that Marcel would not be taken in by the blatant flattery.

In fact Marcel melted in the warmth of the gaze of the attractive English girl.

"Of course, in my position it is up to me to decide what may be revealed and what may not. How can I help? Did I hear you mention Mary Tang? As it happens she was a fellow student when I studied for my degree. I knew her well at that time, though

I'm sure she returned to Hong Kong when she finished here."

"Do you happen to know where she stayed while she was here?" Abby leaned forward giving the besotted Marcel a better view of her cleavage, as she dropped her voice to prevent anyone else from overhearing her question.

"Of course, she was a regular partygoer, very popular, you understand. I visited her apartment on several occasions. It was on the left bank, just walking distance from here." He picked up a pencil and scribbled the address on a piece of paper. He slid it over to Abby who was looking into his eyes.

Abby breathed, "Thank you so much." And picking up the paper, she nodded to Donny. Together they left.

Behind his desk, Marcel Albert sighed, 'Ah... If only...'

Outside Donny looked at Abby with new respect. "He was nearly drooling," he said with a smile. "I never thought I would see that from you."

Abby looked at him. "I'm not made of porcelain, you know, and I'm well aware of the advantages and disadvantages of being a woman. Are you upset?"

Donny thought for a moment. "I thought I was, but do you know I'm not. I'm proud of you. You got co-operation from that little swine that no one else could. Just by showing a little"... he hesitated...... "Initiative?"

Abby burst out laughing and a relieved Donny joined in. For a moment there he thought he had put his foot in it. "By the way I think we should forget the cousins this time. See them next time maybe?"

The pair set off up the road to seek the address Marcel had given them.

Chapter Six

Marak was unhappy. His men had lost sight of the Chinese man and they were casting about like idiots with no idea where to begin seriously looking. He called Peter Carver in and sat looking at the tall Russian with his frog-like eyes.

"Recall that bunch of incompetent idiots. Let us take a logical look at the problem of finding this man. I understand that he was no longer alone when he got away at Le Havre. The chances are he has disposed of the girl by now, but we cannot discount her. If she is still with him, is she also Chinese? If she is, then perhaps we have two strangers in a strange land."

He stopped and smiled. "That sounded like a book I once read." He quoted "*Strangers in a strange land.* There could be a problem, and I suspect it could arise with the girl. Suppose she is not a stranger. Even if she is Chinese she could be one of the many who come here to study.

"Take a look at the Sorbonne. Find out if they have a list of Chinese students for the past six years. Then let us see if any are still here or have just returned."

With just these few words 'The Frog' changed Marcel Albert's life forever, and spoiled Peter Carver's day.

"We do not give out information of former students without their specific permission."

It was satisfying for Marcel to tell this hulking great foreigner to bugger off. Still entranced by his dreams of possibly possessing Abby, he had been interrupted by this big fool asking about former Chinese students.

He became suddenly aware that large sums of money were being pushed under the grill that protected him from irate member of the public. He caught a glimpse of the clutch of thousand euro notes amongst the others and decided to co-operate. Sweeping the notes into the drawer of his desk he forced a smile. "Let me see if I can help you with your problem," he said appeasingly. "Chinese, you say?"

He started looking through his file cards from an index he rescued from beneath the desk. "Strange you should be looking for a Chinese student. I was asked about a girl only this morning. Her friends were looking to her for advice on living and studying here. I told them her old address and off they went quite happy, apparently."

He started to prattle on when he became aware of the closeness of his audience. The hand that slid under the grill and stopped him checking the cards was not friendly. In fact it hurt as it gripped his wrist. "Stop it. That hurts," he said.

"Who wanted to know about the Chinese girl today?" The voice was icy.

"Why, it was a young English couple, a young man and his girlfriend."

"When?" The question snapped back.

"About a half-hour ago. I gave them the address of Mary Tang. She was at college with me several years ago. She probably doesn't live there any more anyway."

"What was the address? Quickly now!"

Marcel Albert was hurting badly now. He wrenched his hand away from the painful grip.

"Who do you think you are?" He shouted.

Another wad of notes came under the screen. "Now then, just give me the address and I'll go away and you can forget you ever saw me."

Rubbing his wrist Marcel swept the extra notes into the drawer. He gave the address from memory.

The visitor hesitated and looked around. There were several people in the area. He swung around and left the building, leaving a worried man behind him. Marcel had no idea how near he had come to losing everything, including his life. Peter thought ruefully he would never have passed out so much money if he had not expected to take it back again.

Marcel put up the sign closing the office and locked the door. Now completely alone, he took the money from the drawer and counted it quickly. Ten thousand euros. Suddenly the plans he had made were achievable. He wouldn't bother his wife with them. She enjoyed being at home with her mother, living just down the road.

Hardly daring to believe he was doing this, he reached into his locker and retrieved his escape kit, a smart Nike sports bag. It was already packed with the basic essentials for an unattached, young man on a singles holiday in the South of France. He had been meaning to leave his bitch of a wife for the past three years. Now he had enough money to make a beginning elsewhere. He had a bank account she knew nothing about and he had been saving ever since he had made his mind up three years ago. With the extra money from today he could afford the share of a boat at Antibes. He could live the life he had always dreamed of.

With his bag and his dreams he left the Sorbonne for the last time, through the south door.

Donny and Abby walked up to the apartment block, which was in fact a tall 19th Century town house. It had been extended and turned into apartments. The locality, spoke money, and though the building was old, the concierge was not. He was young and looked fit. Abby discreetly loosened the top button of her blouse once more as they approached the small desk on the foyer.

She need not have bothered. The young man was more interested in Donny than her. Her shrug said it all, and she refastened her blouse.

Donny smiled. "We were looking for Mary Tang," he said. "She did say she would be coming back to Paris." We guessed that she would end up here again. Can you help?"

The young man smiled at Donny, ignoring Abby and said, "I have not seen her today, but my opposite number who shares this job, said she came in with a friend last night."

"Is it alright if we go straight up to the apartment?" Donny asked hopefully.

Abby interjected at that point, "Oh, come on, Donny. We'll just have to come back when we have spoken to her." She tugged at his sleeve and started to the door.

The concierge, annoyed, turned a frosty look at her. Then smiled at Donny and said, "Same apartment, third floor back. Don't mention me, please." He turned and smirked triumphantly at Abby.

She poked her tongue out at him and raced off up the stairs after Donny.

The apartment was quiet, though there was the sound of music from the apartment opposite.

Donny knocked at the door of opposite apartment. The music stopped and the door was opened by a shapely young woman with a violin in her hand.

"Sorry to bother you. We were looking for Mary Tang. Is she in?"

The violinist looked at Donny for a moment, liked what she saw and said, "If she is she'll be in that apartment, not this one." She stepped out of her door and walked over the landing and banged on the door opposite. "Wake up, Mary. There's a handsome man here to see you."

She grinned wickedly and added quietly, "With a chick in tow."

She spun round and dashed back into her apartment. The sound of the violin started once more.

Mary Tang looked at them. They were inside by now, seated in the lounge. "So what brings you looking for me?"

Abby spoke, "Why should we be looking for you? It could be John Ling we are looking for."

At the mention of the name Mary could not stop herself from showing her surprise. "How... where ... So how do you know about John? I've told no one anything about him."

Donny looked at her gravely. "If he is here, he is in danger, as are you. We are not sure how closely we are followed but you can depend on it that it is only a matter of time. We were given this address by the secretary at the Sorbonne. He said he was in college when you were there. Marcel Albert. I think it was."

"He was a creep. I never did like him." Mary looked worried.

"If you and John Ling are staying here, I suggest you move pronto. The people chasing you are not friendly. Is John here now?"

"No, he had to go and see someone at the Chinese Embassy."

There was a knock at the door. Mary looked through the spy-hole and then opened the door to let a tall Chinese man in.

He did not see Donny and Abby and he said as he walked in, "There are two people asking about you." He stopped as he saw Donny and Abby.

"Who are you? What are you doing here?"

"Probably saving your neck." Donny responded crisply.

There was a knock at the door. Everybody froze on the spot. Then the voice of the concierge came faintly through the panel, "There are men here, with g......"

The words trailed off with a gasp.

All four people within the apartment looked at each other.

Donny and Abby drew their guns and turned to face the door. "Is there another way out of here?" Abby asked.

Mary said in a frightened voice, "The fire escape," and she turned to point through the door into the kitchen.

"I'll go." Abby said to Donny. Turning to John Ling she said, "Have you got a gun?"

With a start he snapped out of the shocked state that the sudden events had induced and nodded. "Yes, in my bag. He ran over to the settee and reached behind it. The bag was a small backpack. The Makarov pistol looked huge, but he checked the magazine, and cocked it, as if he knew what he was doing. "Stay with Donny!" Abby ordered and, nodding to Mary, went into the kitchen to the fire escape.

The opened window revealed the iron stairway down to a small garden at the rear of the house. There was a fence and an alley that ran behind the row of houses.

From the other room there came the sound of a crash as the door was attacked from outside. The key had been tried but the deadbolt had been set. The lock would not open while the bolt was set from the inside of the apartment. Another impact shook the door in its frame.

Abby and Mary went down the fire escape. They got out of the garden and ran along the alley to the roadway at the end. Telling Mary to stay out of sight, Abby walked along to the corner and scanned the street outside the front entrance to the apartments. The Audi was sitting, parked at the door with the engine running. The driver was watching the entrance to the building intently.

Abby heard shots faintly above the other noises of the city. She crossed the road and approached the car from the passenger's side. With gun ready, she swiftly pulled open the passenger door and slid into the car, gun rammed firmly to the temple of the startled driver.

"Out?" She said. "Now!"

The man fumbled with then door and got out. Keeping her gun on him, she slid out of the other door and came round the car. The street was quiet, no one had raised the alarm.

"Open the trunk." Abby ordered.

In the space lay two automatic shotguns, and a box of ammunition.

Abby called Mary over," Take these into the lobby," she indicated the guns and the box. To the driver she said "Weapons!" When he had cautiously given over his belt gun and the ankle weapon, she frisked him, took his wallet and said, "Inside."

She slammed the trunk lid with the driver inside and entered the foyer, where Mary stood ready with a shotgun cocked and ready. She hardly needed the laconic comment, "Skeet shooting," to know that Mary was competent with the weapon. Picking up the other shotgun, she led the way up the stairs.

On the landing of the second story two people were whispering, looking up to the landing above them. The middle-aged lady looked scared. The old man with her was trying to find a code on his cell phone, but his fingers were clumsy and he kept fumbling and muttering.

Abby took the phone from his hands and flung it down the stairwell as the two girls, with guns ready, passed on up the stairs to the third floor. There were three men upright and one on the floor with a bloody head. The door was splintered where bullets had passed through in both directions.

Abby looked at the conscious men. All were looking toward the splintered door. She raised the shotgun and fired into the wall between the three men, shouting at the same time. "Drop the weapons!" Racking another shell into the chamber to emphasis the order.

The three men turned, one lifting his gun as he swung round. Mary's shotgun fired. Astonished, the man folded in the middle and collapsed in a bloody mess on the floor.

The other two dropped their guns as if they were burning hot. They clattered to the floor.

Abby called out, "Donny, we're all clear out here. Mary and I have the men under our guns."

The door opened slowly. A mirror appeared. For a moment nothing else happened, then Donny came out followed by John Ling. "What kept you?" Donny grinned and looked at the carnage. The concierge groaned as he came round, his head bloody but obviously not too serious.

Donny turned to John and Mary, "Get your things. You cannot stay here now." He gestured to the two survivors to pick up their companion and bring him in to the apartment. He then searched them and relieved them of their extra weapons and wallets; tying them with adhesive tape in the few minutes it needed for Mary and John to collect their gear together.

Taking the collection of money from all the wallets, they left the gunmen and their dead companion, and closed the splintered door once more. They helped the battered concierge down the stairway where they left him with the lady on the floor below. The Audi was still parked outside. The driver was still where they had left him. Releasing him from the trunk, they left him to help his friends. Having added the contents of the driver's wallet and the extra guns to their haul, they drove off down the street. There was still no sign of activity despite the racket caused by the battle that had just taken place.

Abby called Jonathon as they drove, "We will not come to the apartment. We have two friends with us. Do you think Isobel can help here?"

Jonathon gave her the number and Abby rang Isobel. As a result they drove to a garage north of the river, where the shutter opened as they approached and closed as soon as the car passed the threshold. Inside the double garage was a Mercedes 320 series in silver and in the end wall was a stairway. As they entered the stairway a voice spoke, directing them to the basement apartment where Isobel waited.

Donny and Abby were relieved to find that Jonathon was also there to greet them.

John Ling and Mary Tang were unsure whether they were safe or even further in trouble.

"I have the feeling you have both been conned by a bunch of rogue agents formerly employed by the CIA." Jonathon's voice was calm and even. "In the circumstances I would like to propose we pool all the information we have on this matter. It is quite clear that there are things we have not been told but we may be able to deduce something from our pooled knowledge."

"I thought the issue was all about plates for forging U.S. one hundred dollar bills and the paper to print them on." Donny opened the discussion with this comment, which puzzled John Ling.

"Where did that idea come from? Forgeries? What is that all about?"

Jonathon smiled quietly, "I'm afraid that is the story put about by your presumed bosses at CIA. We now know that there is no genuine CIA input involved."

Mary Tang said, "The people who sent me along said they..." She stopped and thought for a moment. "They didn't say they were. I just presumed they were CIA."

"So, who the blazes are they? Why all the cloak and dagger intrigue over the smuggling of John Ling into Europe? Who are you?" Abby turned to the Chinese man sitting across the table.

"I am just a Chinese patriot. I have been unjustly imprisoned by the current totalitarian government. I was released under conditions that essentially prevented me participating in political activities, and thus contacting the vast mass of the Chinese electorate.

"My escape was staged by members of the political party who support me. I believe the 'so called' CIA people who put Mary in with me have been tasked with removing me from the political scene."

"Killing you?"

"I believe so. Happily, Mary and I found mutual survival in our conveyance here. That has resulted in the possibility of our sharing the future together. Our friendship led to the eluding of my followers, certainly temporarily. Though I am troubled by the intervention of the people today."

The others listened to the rather formal English John Ling used with interest. Then Jonathon commented, "Make no mistake, please. Those people involved today were not members of the CIA group. They are in fact criminals. I can almost certainly verify that they were members of a local gang led by a man known as Marak, aka 'The Frog'." Jonathon lifted his hand to stop interruption. "I'll explain later," he continued. "The underworld here has obviously picked up the rumour that the Chinese authorities put about to discredit you. They wish to make you a criminal in the eyes of the people, obviously to reduce your popularity with the people. The attack today was opportunism, based on the Beijing rumors. The attempt today was to capture you, an attempt that got out of hand. The so-called CIA people will kill you in some incriminating way to demonstrate to the Chinese people that you are not a person to be followed in any sense of the word."

"My family will look after us," Mary Tang said out of the blue.

"Your family should be warned. They may use them to make you give up John."

Jonathon leaned forward. "You know their number here? Ring them now!"

Mary jumped up and walked over to the telephone. When it was answered she spoke rapidly in Mandarin. She answered questions once, twice, then smiled and put the phone down. "My parents are safe. They have bodyguards. They have also been contacted by someone from the embassy warning them, so they have increased their security." She smiled.

"My father said he was happy to hear my voice. They wish me to bring John to meet them, when things are back to normal once more."

Chapter Seven

Pierre Marak was angry. The three survivors from the attack on Mary Tang's apartment were sitting facing his fury. They winced as he spluttered and swore at their incompetence. First for failure, second for losing their fellow gunman.

Peter Carver intervened, "But boss, we know the story of the printing plates is garbage. So why are we still chasing these people?"

"The Chinese government will pay through the nose for the man, John Ling. He's a bloody political 'hot potato' and he must be worth a million, at least. Understand?"

Carver nodded thoughtfully, "So what next?"

"Find out where they have gone to ground. I'm sure they won't have gone far. Find them and bring them here to me. Have you understood?" He waited for and received a nod in understanding. Then, calmer now, he sat back and lit a cigar.

Donny and Abby left Isobel's apartment and roamed the area, keeping an eye open for any sign of the Chinese. It was pointless they knew, but they were both fed up with responding to attacks and anxious to go on the offensive.

They returned late in the afternoon unsuccessful and footsore but feeling better because they had been out doing something.

Jonathon rang to tell them that the gang led by Marak was hunting Ling. The word was out to find the Chinese man and the girl. There was a warning that they might be with a young man and woman, believed to be English. They will be armed.

Jonathon told them to stay indoors and keep the Chinese away from the windows. He had spoken to Isobel who passed the message on.

Abby asked "Does he know where the gang is based?"

"Apparently not," Isobel said. "But I think I do." It seemed that she had followed one of her attackers back to a private house. There had been plenty of people about at the time. She really did not know what to do next, so she had withdrawn.

In the Chinese embassy there was turmoil. The entire operation had gone wrong and John Ling was loose and running. The operation depended on his being under control. Wu Fat had been uneasy about the whole idea. His sympathies were with the repressed democrats who were seeking to replace the current rule in China with a freely-elected government. It was not something he could talk about but it was true that, when the opportunity arose, he did nudge things in the right direction. Currently his efforts were concentrated on confusing the efforts of those hunting John Ling. He had been fully aware of the cover story issued by the secretariat. It had not been difficult to deduce what they had in mind once John Ling was captured.

Chen Li had been sent to the embassy in Paris to co-ordinate the operation. He was anxious to succeed and gain prestige within the party. It had made him act too quickly and rashly. The three men he had sent to dispose of Jonathon Glynn's contacts had been themselves disposed of, with considerable loss of face for Chen Li.

Wu Fat knew he was taking a big risk but he considered it was worth it. He left the embassy grounds by the rear entrance. His car was parked within the compound so he had hired a small Kia and parked it where it would blend in with the parked cars of the local Parisians. He slid into the driver's seat, and after carefully looking all around for watchers, he drove off. In a car park near the Pompidou centre, he left the car and walked into the centre.

He used a public telephone to call and when the call was answered he said, "The embassy is issuing a contract on John Ling, Mary Tang, and your two young friends. Though they have not been identified yet, it is only a matter of time. They do have a bad photograph of them both." He placed the phone back on the hook and walked on.

Jonathon replaced the phone on his desk. He wondered who the Chinese was. The man's accent was American, but he was not fooled. The man was Oriental. Only a Chinese would have access to the information the man was passing.

He spoke to Donny and suggested that they needed new disguises. There was a photograph of them going the rounds of the Chinese.

It was an accident. So often these things happen in that way. Candice was a tall willowy blonde, one of Marak's string of prostitutes. Having been visiting a client in the apartment block next door to Isobel's, she had stopped to change her shoes before driving herself back to her own apartment. Seated in the driving seat of her car, she slipped off her high-heeled, working shoes, and replaced them with her flat moccasins for driving. She was parked next to the gate to the basement apartment and glanced up as the apartment door opened. She saw a small group just inside the open door. A Chinese man and girl; they were talking with a white girl with a second man. They were arguing. Then the door closed. Nobody came out. She continued to arrange herself and drove off to the apartment she shared with two of her friends who were in the same business.

When she got there the other two were excitedly discussing the latest edict issued by the 'Frog'. Keep an eye out for a Chinese man and girl, possibly in company of a young man and woman, white, French or at least European.

Candice listened while they explained and when they were finished she thought about it, remembering the group she had seen at the next door apartment block from her client's.

From her room she rang up and spoke to Peter Carver, explaining about her sighting, and gave the address.

He thought about things, but decided not to tell Marak in case it was a false alarm. Calling together his depleted group of men, just five at present, he briefed them on the target and the address. He made sure they were all armed, and they set off in two cars to check the information and if true capture the Chinese. If the two who had rescued the Chinese were there, he would dispose of them at the same time.

Donny and Abby left the apartment by 9.30 am to get different clothing to alter their appearance once more.

At 10.00 am there was a knock on the front door, John and Mary looked at each other. John shrugged, "They have probably forgotten something. Or perhaps Isobel has called......" He stopped abruptly as he opened the door. It slammed back against the wall trapping his hand for the moment. Mary screamed as two men burst in. Both were armed with guns.

When Donny and Abby returned they found a worried Isobel alone in the apartment.

"The door was open when I came down. I saw a car drive off. I think they have been snatched."

"Who by? The mob or the Chinese?"

"I think perhaps the mob," Isobel said. "I think the Chinese would have taken all their things with them; as you can see their stuff is still all over the place."

"Could you recognise the car?" Abby asked.

"Oh, yes. It was easy to remember, an American limo, dark red, local Paris plates."

"You said you had once followed the mob to their base. Shall we take a look?" Donny smiled grimly and retrieved the Walther from his waistband and checked the action and magazine.

The other two followed his lead checking their own guns.

Isobel said, "We might need a little extra firepower." She led the way out into the area, where the steps led up to the street. There was a doorway under the steps which she unlocked. The room was obviously intended for solid fuel from the time when the house had been heated with a coal fired furnace. Now each apartment had its own heating system the furnace was gone, the room cleared and the end wall closed off with double steel doors.

Isobel punched a code into the concealed keypad beside the doors and with a sigh the right-hand door opened.

The area behind the door was about 8ft by 12ft obviously once the store room for the cleaning staff and probably the gardener. It was now shelved and there was a bench along the back wall where an internal stairway had once stood. There was a hatch where the door had once been, now high on the wall, above the bench. The workshop had been converted into a small weapon store since Isobel had returned to Paris, hence the steel doors and keypad lock.

Isobel took an AK-47 down from the shelf and passed it to Donny. She followed it with two loaded magazines. For Abby and herself she found two mini-guns with extended magazines that projected from the pistol grip of the deadly little weapons.

A bag from beneath the bench accommodated the guns, and for good measure she added four tear-smoke grenades. "No masks, I'm afraid. Goggles and a wet handkerchief is the best we can do." She laughed. "At least we will know when they will be going off."

Loaded, they made their way to the car parked around the corner and piled in. Isobel drove.

Donny rang Jonathon and told him what they were doing. Jonathon took the address down and left the office at a run.

Marak's headquarters were at a private house, converted to accommodate his particular needs. The entire second floor was given over to his personal apartment. The ground floor was the office and a room where his men relaxed. There was a small hallway immediately inside the front door. The door on the left opened into the rest room. The stairs to the upper floor were straight ahead. The cellar was behind the door on the right. In the restroom on the left was a pool table, a table and several armchairs. In the corner there was a kitchen area and a fridge/freezer and microwave. The room was occupied by five men sitting around watching the TV, and smoking. Currently the cellar downstairs contained the two Chinese and one trainee in the two cells built into the area. Outside sat a disgruntled gaoler armed with a shotgun.

The trainee, a pretty but un-cooperative, Eurasian girl had been there for some time. She explained to Mary Tang, who shared her cell, that she could survive being raped, but giving herself to men other than her husband would be degrading and against her religious beliefs. "They will need to kill me of course, but that would be better than being raped daily by these disgusting men."

Horrified, Mary sat beside her and listened. The girl's name was Jeanne, and she had been kidnapped in Lyon and sold to Marak's organisation with several other girls. They had all submitted. Some willingly, and she presumed put to work on the streets. She had survived for three weeks so far. There had been several breaks in the training and the so-called instructors had changed twice since she had arrived.

John Ling was depressed. He had been informed that they were to be sold to the Chinese embassy as soon as a deal could be arranged. Gloomily he thought over all the problems he and his friends had faced. All stage-managed from the start. All set up to discredit his people. He almost gave in to despair.

With an effort, he recalled Isobel saying she had once followed the gang to their base. Perhaps, he thought, just perhaps, she or Donny might be able to do something.

It seemed ages since they had been placed in their cells. They were in walled rooms with barred doors to allow their jailors to see them. Unfortunately it was difficult to communicate as the walls were thick and their voices could be heard by the watcher. John knew that Mary was in with another girl prisoner. He had seen her when they were brought down and thrust into their rooms. Without any real idea in mind he called out to the next cell.

"Are you alright, Mary?"

The guard said, "Shut up, pig."

Mary called back, "We are alright. Watch the guard though. My friend here says he likes men, not women."

"Shut up, bitch, or I will come in there and show you how I hate women." The jailor was annoyed at being here with the prisoners. He was not pretty. His scarred face was evidence of the smallpox he had suffered from in his youth. Girls sneered when he approached them, so he hated them. *Damn! The man was at it again,* he thought. Picking up the shotgun beside his chair he went to the man's cell door. The man was calling to his girlfriend next door.

The gaoler shouted in turn, "Shut up, I said." He lifted the shotgun and poked it through the bars at the man inside. John grabbed the twin barrels and yanked the gun from his grip pulling him close to the bars at the same time. John's other hand gripped his captor's throat, the Tae-kwon-do hardened hand throttling the man where he stood frantically trying to loosen the killing grip.

John thrust the gun behind him on the floor and with his other hand, reinforced his grip on the man's throat. The struggle did not last. The man sagged, his face suffused and swollen. John allowed the body to slump to the floor, reaching and capturing the keys chained to the man's belt. The key to his cell was the fourth one he tried, and with a sigh of relief, he opened the door and stepped out. The dead man had an automatic thrust in the back of his waistband, John took it and placed it with the shotgun on the chair the gaoler had used.

Then he opened the other cell and released the girls. Mary introduced him to her fellow prisoner, Jeanne. John was pleased to see that she was also quite calm and not at all put out by the dead man on the floor. Between them they manoeuvred the heavy body into the chair, propping him up into as lifelike a position as they could manage.

"Now we wait," he said. "There are too many men up there for us to tackle with just two weapons. Wait in the cell with the door unlocked so that if anyone looks, things will appear normal. If anyone comes in I'll try and capture him. That should give us at least one more gun and a better chance against the men in there." He nodded at the doorway. They returned to their unlocked cells and waited to see what would happen.

John was resigned to the possibility that they would all die, but at least they would take some of their captors with them.

Donny watched the house with interest. It was a post-war building with steel-framed windows. It lay back from the road behind a low hedge. There was no room for a driveway and the big Ford limo was parked on the street outside.

There was a watcher behind the hedge in a chair, the warm sunshine allowing him to work on his tan and incidentally doze off from time to time. After all no-one would dare start anything here. All the locals knew this was mob territory.

While Donny watched three men came out of the house, got into the Ford and drove off, exchanging rude comments with the watcher at the door.

"Probably at least three inside and one in front." Donny turned to the others. "Shall we?"

Isobel and Abby nodded.

Chapter Eight

Abby strolled across the road and looked over the hedge at the man lolling in the chair outside the door. "Do you speak English?"

"I certainly do, M'selle."

"Good. Put your hands up, please. Place your hands on your head and walk over to the car across the road where my two friends have their guns pointing at you."

The man was relieved of his two weapons and questioned about the people in the house. He was quite cooperative (especially when he realized that Isobel was one of the two in the car).

"The boss is upstairs with his woman. There are two in the downstairs rest area and one in the basement with the prisoners."

"What prisoners are there in the basement?" Donny asked.

"One girl in training and two Chinese, a man and a girl. They are in the two cells there. The guard has the keys."

Safely tucked in the trunk of the car, the protesting prisoner was secured while the three rescuers crossed the road. They tried the front door of the house. There was no problem getting in. The door was not locked so the three entered the hallway, un-challenged. From the doorway on the left side came the sound of a TV. On the right there was another door that they had established led to the cellar.

Donny and Abby opened the cellar door while Isobel took station outside the other door, just in case of interference from the men inside.

The stair down to the cellar was clear. The cell doors were in view though there was no one in plain sight at the moment.

They crept down the stairs and peered round the corner at the sleeping guard. He looked odd to Donny. Reaching round he tapped the man on the shoulder with the barrel of his gun.

The man slumped to the floor in a heap. The voice from the nearest cell said "Stay where you are and don't move."

Abby said, "Some people just are too impatient. Hullo, John. It's Donny and Abby. We have come to rescue you, though we are obviously wasting our time."

John Ling appeared, carrying the guard's shot-gun. He called to the next cell. "Come out, girls. Our ride has arrived."

Mary Tang and Jeanne appeared from the other cell.

"Are you all okay? Have they harmed you at all?"

"They were saving that for later," John said. "We are all ready to go whenever you are."

Donny grinned. "Let's go." He turned and led the way up the stairs, and cautiously opened the door. Isobel was there, still poised with her gun ready. He joined her and whispered, "Take a look outside and see if the coast is clear."

Isobel nodded and went to the front door. Having looked through the letter box, she opened the door and looked again before she waved them out through the door and across the road to the waiting car.

Back at the apartment building, the group moved up to Isobel's old apartment on the top floor with the view of the river. The basement apartment was advertised for rent with a sign outside to publicize the fact that they had moved on.

In the headquarters of Philippe Marak, the atmosphere was strained. The discovery of the loss of all three prisoners had caused the gang leader to lose his temper. The result was that even more losses had occurred to the shrinking group of men. The desertion of the two men who had not been aware of the activities of the rescuers had followed the wounding of one of the men, shot by their enraged leader.

When added to the loss of the door-guard and the death of the gaoler, Marak's force had been reduced to three men, only one of whom he could trust.

Peter Carver had served Philippe Marak for well over a year and, during that time, performed many tasks that others might have found odd and bizarre. The peculiarities of his boss's preferences had never really bothered Peter. He himself had likes and dislikes that others may not have approved of, and in an odd way his tolerances extended far beyond what would have been expected or accepted by morally upright citizens.

When his boss suggested that the removal of the two young people, now believed to be British, would be a good step towards recapturing the two Chinese, he found himself oddly reluctant to agree. It was not because he was squeamish. He had killed before on several occasions. It was something to do with the fact that the two young people concerned were in no way criminals. They had no record of committing any crime. Their actions so far had all been in response to attacks upon themselves and others in their company. All Peter's previous efforts had involved crooks and frauds of various kinds, people that may not have had criminal records, but had their noses firmly in the trough of venality and corruption, feeding off the misfortune of others.

His expressed reluctance to undertake the task caused Marak to begin to consider replacing him. "You do not agree with me over the removal of the British pair from the scene? What is wrong?"

"Boss, they are just a couple of kids. What can they do? Why should we bother with them? We can manage whether they live or die. I have never liked killing for the sake of it."

Marak considered this new development, holding back the fury that built up in him at being defied in this way. "So, you do not want to kill them?" He forced a smile, "OK, I'll cancel the order, and I await your suggestions for getting around them without killing them with interest."

His sarcasm was lost on Peter, whose French verbal skills still lacked the finesse of the educated, fluent speaker.

Marak, having dismissed his right-hand man, thought for a while. Then he picked up the telephone beside his chair and made a call.

Peter may not have had the conversational skills to understand the sarcastic barbs of his leader, but he did know his boss well enough to question something when his boss acted out of character. He had expected a violent reaction to his objection to the killing of the youngsters. The calm acceptance of his words had surprised and at first pleased him. On thinking about it afterwards, however, he realised that this was not Marak's way.

In the apartment, John Ling was seated at the window watching the street below. When the figure of Peter Carver appeared he started up, calling a warning to the others seated around the room. They gathered around the window concealed by the net curtains and watched as Peter looked around. He dived down the steps to the basement apartment and put something through the door. He departed walking swiftly away, head swinging from side to side as if he were checking for watchers.

As he walked around the corner another figure appeared, a camera slung round his neck, and casually strolled along the street, he rounded the same corner as Peter Carver used and disappeared.

"What do you make of that?" John said.

"I think we need to see what he put through the door downstairs. Isobel, when does the new tenant arrive?"

"In three days time, I still have the keys."

"Good. Let us find out what he left and see what he was up to."

Donny took the keys from Isobel and left the apartment. Abby followed a few seconds later to cover his back, if needed. The habits learned over the past two years were well ingrained.

They returned to their waiting companions a few minutes later, note in hand.

Donny handed it to Isobel. "What do you make of this?"

She read it and passed it to John. Mary read it over John's shoulder.

"How odd! He seems to be a different person to the one I imagined. Do you think this is part of some devious plan to split us up and make it easier to capture us?" Mary was no fool. The former flighty butterfly was gone and the keen brain, under-used up to now, was beginning to get into its stride at last.

"I think this is genuine." Isobel was quite serious. "And I think this man is marked for removal by his boss. For his sake, I hope he has made arrangements to get out of Paris in a hurry."

"You really believe this?" Abby said hesitantly,

"I certainly do. From all the things I have learned since this business started, my impression is that Marak, his boss, is a mean, vicious, twisted man with about as much compassion as a plank. The note says that Marak has put out a contract on you both." She nodded at Donny and Abby. "My guess is that Peter, is ... ?" At Donny's nod she continued, "Peter is also marked for replacement. He either leaves Paris or, he removes Marak."

Peter Carver was packed and ready to leave, when the knock came at the door to his small apartment. The area of St Denis was not one where salesmen called nor did neighbours pop in for a social chat and a coffee. He picked up his favorite weapon from the table beside him. The big Colt 9mm automatic felt reassuring in his hand. He slid the action open and closed, popping the loaded cartridge out, catching it in his ready hand. The magazine slipped easily from the butt and he pressed the rejected bullet into the magazine and reinserted it.

He pulled back the hammer, and went to the door in response to the second knock.

The small screen that received the picture of the landing outside his door revealed the small figure of a girl. He recognized her as one of the string operated by Marak. He also recognized her as a friend.

He opened the door. "Magda?"

"Peter. You must leave here quickly."

"Why, Magda? What is wrong?"

"Charon was with me. He has been hired for two jobs by the Frog. He said he would do them first, then you."

"Did he know you were my friend?"

She shivered. "I think so. He looked very knowing and he was rough with me." A tear leaked from the corner of her eye smearing the mascara, tracking a black streak down her face.

"Oh, Peter, he is bad. He has killed so many people. He boasts about it. He says the more people know the easier it is to kill them. They panic and stop thinking straight."

"I will deal with it. Magda, it is time. Stay here until I return. I will be back. You may depend on it. We will make our plans then, if you agree?"

She looked up at him. "Oh, Peter, you know I will. I will be here waiting."

Peter kissed her quickly and left. He considered his odds of survival roughly 60-40, only because he was warned and therefore looking for his assassin, He did not believe for one second that he was number two in line. Charon, knowing Magda was his friend, had fed her that information deliberately.

Despite being warned about him, Charon almost caught him by surprise. The flicker of movement in corner of his eye followed by the muzzle flash sent him instinctively into a forward roll, gun in hand and ready, despite the tug he felt in his right side.

He swore. He knew he had been hit. From his position on the ground he could see the approaching feet of his attacker under the car parked beside him. He lined up the Colt and squeezed the trigger. He smiled as the near ankle shattered. The scream of his victim rang out as the rest of the man's body came into view. The gun in his right hand confirmed Peter's judgement. He fired again as the man's gun swung toward him. The bullet struck Charon's fancy, silver-plated gun, the pieces of plated steel from the broken weapon were blown back into the face of its owner. His scream cut off abruptly as a piece of the metal went through his right eye and buried itself in his brain. He died!

Peter levered himself to his feet. The pain was kicking in. The initial shock of the wound had worn off. He felt the wetness of the blood at his side. Opening his jacket he could see the patch of blood-soaked shirt where the bullet had scraped a rib from the feel of it. He gathered the shirt and wadded the tail against the wound. His tie was long enough to hold the improvised dressing in place. Looking around the silent street, he smiled grimly. This was after all St Denis, the people here did not want to be part of any shooting. He got into the car carefully, and with difficulty. He drove to Marak's house. It was 10.15pm. The door guard was inside.

Peter parked the car and, ignoring the front door, made his way round to the side of the house. The bolt hole was in the side wall, concealed by a turf covered trapdoor. The effort of lifting it nearly caused Peter to faint.

Leaving the trapdoor open, he made his way down the steps down to the specially made doorway. The steel door there was shut. The handle was a trap for the unwary. It would only operate if it was pulled out and twisted the correct way. Marak refused to depend on anything electric or electronic on his escape hatch. For Peter it opened, and he was inside Marak's house.

The other men within the house were with the exception of one, all new.

He looked at himself. The bloody mess on his left side had dried to some extent, though the effort of lifting the trapdoor had created a new damp patch.

With a shrug he checked his weapon, sliding the full magazine home and cocking it. The stair ended at a narrow passage that sloped upwards alongside the back wall of the house. At the end, a sliding panel in the en-suite bathroom of Marak's apartment allowed the occupier concealed entry or exit at will.

The bathroom was empty though he could the murmur of voices from the room below. He put the gun down beside the sink and drew a glass of water. He drank thirstily, then again. He took the gun up once more and opened the door to the bedroom next door. Peter crept across the bedroom to the lounge door that was partly open, the shaft of light coming through the gap making visibility possible in the semi-dark of the bedroom.

He made it to the door and leaned against the wall to get his breath back. He was feeling the effect of the wound he had suffered earlier. The weight of the gun in his hand was comforting, but it was also tiring.

Finally he straightened, and with the gun hanging down by his side, he walked through the door into Pierre Marak's lounge.

Marak saw him. He was seated at the desk in the corner. He reacted and reached for the panic button. He stopped as the gun lifted. Peter wagged it and indicated the chair on the other side of the desk.

Pierre Marak began to sweat. He moved over as instructed. Then he removed the gun from under his arm and with two fingers placed in on the table in front of him. He pushed it across the table and it dropped to the carpet. As it tipped over the edge he reached for the gun in his ankle holster. Peter shot him in the gun arm. The small gun failed to clear the holster completely and it dropped from the nerveless fingers and joined the other gun on the carpet. There was a sudden rush of feet from downstairs as the sound of the gunfire was heard.

Peter lifted the gun once more and nodded to Marak once more.

Marak swore clutching his bleeding arm, but he shouted to the men outside, "Get the hell out. I fired my gun by mistake. So bugger off; all of you."

The noise outside stopped and then it was followed by the sound of the men descending the stairs.

Peter looked at Marak. "Why?"

Marak said, "You know too much. It is simpler to make sure of these things. You should know me by now."

"I was hoping I was wrong," Peter said. He walked round the desk and twitched open the drawer that Marak used for day-to-day payouts. It slid smoothly open and he swept up the bundle of notes lying there, stuffing them in his pockets. He returned to the door of the bathroom, his pockets bulging. For a moment he looked into the furious face of his boss. "Goodbye, Pierre." The noise of the shot created another rush of noise from downstairs.

The door slid open. He closed it firmly. The trapdoor dropped into place behind him.

He parked away from the apartment and made his way there through the underground garage on foot. Magda was waiting, anxious and concerned when she saw the blood on his jacket.

Peter stripped off his jacket and the torn shirt. With the help of Magda, the wound was washed and dressed. She taped the lips of the tear together, placed a pad over the area, and then more tape to hold it all in place.

While Peter rested, she packed a suitcase for him and then helped him dress in clean shirt. She transferred the stuff in his pockets to another jacket.

Peter, still a little woozy but feeling much better, collected spare ammunition and dumped it into another bag along with Marak's money and his own emergency cash and passports.

"We will buy what you need when we get out of Paris." He took Magda's anxious face in his hands. "You saved my life," he said, and kissed her gently on the lips, then taking her hand hoisted one of the bags in the other. Magda collected the second bag, and they left the apartment for the last time.

Chapter Nine

In the Chinese Embassy there was silence in the room dedicated to the Social Affairs Department,(SAD).

The group sitting around the long table had just been made aware of the news involving the demise of Pierre Marak and the effective dispersal of his organization. While it seemed that the leadership would naturally devolve onto Peter Carver, the Russian, he himself had disappeared. There was vague rumor that it had been Peter Carver who had been responsible for Marak's death, though as yet there was no confirmation.

Wu Fat had been involved in the collection of this information. He knew, in fact, that Peter Carver had boarded the train to the south two hours after the killing had occurred.

His reasons for keeping the information to himself were complex. But in view of his disapproval of this entire elaborate scam operation set up to defame a man he admired, he was unwilling to do anything to further the plans of these idiots.

The Chairman, Chen Li, sent to Paris by SAD headquarters in Beijing, spoke quietly. His voice carried the full length of the long table, and all the people seated listened with close attention. Failure to understand instructions was not an acceptable excuse. In fact, excuses were not accepted, period. "We were in negotiation with this man, Marak, for the capture of John Ling and Mary Tang. Here in Paris it has been awkward for our people to operate without arousing interest in our affairs. It was therefore sensible to employ local talent for the task. Now it seems that local talent is no longer available. I do not wish to brief another group of foreigners, so we are left to us our own resources in this affair."

He faced Wu Fat. "Sir, you are the local director of field operations here. Are there any suggestions you can make in this matter?"

Greatly daring, despite his high position in SAD, Wu Fat took a calculated risk. "You honour me, Chen Li, but I am not optimistic about our chances in this matter. We have lost men already, causing considerable embarrassment to our Ambassador here. John Ling and his partner have obviously received assistance from local people, possibly from EU intelligence. Without the assistance of westerners, we are going to be handicapped in our search simply because our people stand out. I recommend we abort this operation and allow John Ling to run free until he returns to China. He is after all only of significance there. Here he is just another dissident from the other side of the world."

There were several sharp intakes of breath among the people seated around the table at the temerity of Wu Fat's suggestion. All heads turned to the head of the table.

For a moment Wu Fat thought he might have done it. The brief look of uncertainty on Chen Li's face was all he noticed until the face hardened into his normal impassive set. "I wish to know about the two British people who keep interfering with our plans."

Wu Fat for a moment considered pointing out that the unprovoked attack had been made upon the two British people, not the other way round. He could also have commented that the same attack had brought them into the conflict for the first time. Wisely he kept all these thoughts to himself. They were things that could be mentioned in private but it would entail serious loss of face if they were mentioned in public.

Instructions were issued for an approach to be made to one of the other gangs in Paris to see if men could be recruited to carry out local jobs without implicating the Embassy. On a much more serious note, a suggestion was made to hire a detective agency to locate the whereabouts of the British couple. They could then be dealt with at leisure.

For Wu Fat this was all bad news. His own superiors in Paris were powerless to interfere with this exercise. Originating as it had in Beijing, the power behind the operation was way above the pay grade of the Ambassador himself.

There was little he could do but contact Jonathon Glynn once more and that required special arrangements. Here was a problem, as the current security clampdown meant that each of the senior staff at the embassy was shadowed for their own protection.

First he decided to speak to his own contacts in Beijing. The visiting team had arrived without prior warning. Though he knew Chen Li occupied a senior position in the SAD, he was in fact junior to Wu Fat in rank. His fanatical hatred of the Democratic movement was public knowledge at home, and many people were scared of him. It had allowed him to get away with acts that others could not even contemplate.

Over the secure line to his father, Wu Fat discovered that Chen Li was not in fact under orders from Beijing. He was in Paris on the nod of the Director. There was no official authority for this operation. If he succeeded in his plan, he would survive. If he failed, his career was over.

As head of station for the SAD in Paris, Wu Fat was responsible for all that occurred here in the name of the SAD.

He spoke with the Ambassador, explaining the situation as his father had given it to him. What was happening was an attempt to save the career of Chen

Li, at the expense of the careers of both Wu Fat and the Ambassador.

The result was that both of their positions were in hazard if things went wrong. The Ambassador was willing to back the actions Wu Fat was contemplating. It had been a relief to discover that, in addition, the Ambassador was firmly committed to free elections and would be happy if the current operation should fail.

The Ambassador was called to the Élysée Palace for a chat with the French President. It was not an unusual occurrence. The meeting was also attended by ambassadors from several other nations represented in the diplomatic circle in Paris. All those present were accompanied by close staff members, and it was the custom of the Chinese delegation to vary the entourage as the Élysée was renowned for its exquisite cuisine. The presence of Wu Fat in the party was not unusual.

With the British party Jonathon Glynn was included due to the absence, owing to illness, of his nominal boss.

The discussion between Wu Fat and Jonathon Glynn would have baffled a listener with the sheer banality of their conversation. In fact, the two men were both skilled in the art of misdirection. Communication was conducted in nuance, expression and tacit understanding of the subject and object of their conversation. Wu Fat's last words before turning to speak to the others present was the silent 'good luck', lip-read by Jonathon during the parting handshake. The notes were exchanged with the handshake.

Back in his office Jonathon read the note once more, then tuned to his computer and typed in the names of Wu Fat and Chen Li.

Wu Fat had started his adult career involved in the political manoeuvrings of the eighties. He survived to become a member of the diplomatic service after obtaining his degree from the university in Shanghai. He was sent to take a course in English at university in Hong Kong, the course obviously combined with an introduction into information gathering in a comparatively easy environment.

He then disappeared from view for several years, finally reappearing in the UN delegation in New York. His promotion was steady rather than dramatic, though he was credited with several small coups over the period. His sympathies were judged to be progressively democratic, favouring increasing freedom of speech and extension of the power of the people rather than the maintenance of the current autocracy.

Chen Li was a different matter. His youth had been one of ruthless support for the establishment. It was a career littered with acts of brutal repression and cynical career enhancement at the expense of others. Until recently his services had earned him the support and the approval of his masters, the extreme element in the administration. However, during his last two operations in Tibet and then in Sin Kiang, he had fallen out of favor. Whilst the government were anxious to maintain their power, politics required at least a nod at progression towards more democratic rule. World trade and the increasing wealth of the country demanded that a softer image be presented. Chen Li did not work that way and had, as a result, upset his backers to the extent that his future was in doubt.

Typically he had initiated this current scheme to blacken the name of a very much admired member of the opposition, who held no official position, but in the event of free election, would come out in an extremely powerful position. Also typically, his plans were based on direct method rather than finesse. The team he had brought were all known to him and accustomed to getting their way in their homeland. They were not really suited for operating in France.

Jonathon sat back and thought about it. The note lay on the desk in front of him. Idly he picked it up and read it once more.

The group under Chen Li are here to destroy the reputation of, then kill, John Ling. They hold no official position and are not protected by diplomatic immunity. The Ambassador and I have no authority over them. Keeping John Ling away from them will

be enough, if that is possible. They know of your friends and will kill them without mercy or warning.

The note was unsigned.

With a sigh Jonathon rose from his desk and picked up the note. He copied it and put the original in a file drawer, which he locked. Then collecting the copy he left the office, taking care to lock the door on his way out.

At the apartment the others were becoming restless. The summer weather outside did not help, and even though there was the rooftop patio they could use, the lure of the river was there with the gallery and the shops. Saturday was proving stressful for them all.

Having suffered from the hints and sighs all morning, Donny and John gave in and agreed to take the party for lunch on the Bateaux-Mouches, the restaurant boats that sailed the River Seine providing meals at the weekend while cruising through the Parisian landscape.

At the insistence of the two men, the women all went in disguise and travelled together. The two men, also in their disguises, shared a second taxi to the river terminal near the Pont de l'Alma, beside the Élysée Palace. There was no problem. They had managed to book by telephone, and having boarded in time, they were soon relaxing and enjoying the trip.

Jonathon found them as they came ashore. He was unhappy to put it mildly, though he kept his displeasure to himself until they returned to the apartment.

When they read the note, they started to ask questions all at once.

Jonathon held up both hands in protest. "Listen, I have no reason to disbelieve that note. It came to me personally from a member of the Chinese Embassy. As far as we know he is the SAD agent in charge here in Paris. He told me that he is a supporter of the movement for free voting in China, and will have no part in framing you. He was the man who tipped us off about Marak and his gang. Unfortunately he cannot take any action from his end as the man, Chen Li, has powerful backing at home in China. If we just keep the man at bay for a while the problem will go away."

"How can I do that?" John said, "I cannot just go into hiding indefinitely!"

"We may have the answer to that." Abby said. She looked at Donny. He shrugged "Why not? We have a boat, currently moored at Boulogne. How would you like a summer cruise up the coast to Holland, perhaps through the Kiel Canal into the Baltic. Abby and I had been planning a cruise when this party started. If you like the idea we can go and lose ourselves for a month or so."

Mary Tang spoke for the first time. "John, I would like to visit my parents, but to be honest, I don't dare. At the moment the risk is too great. I would be happy to go for a cruise until things ease off. How about it?"

John smiled. "What can I say? You have all been so kind, helping us and risking your lives for us. I would be delighted to come sailing with you."

All eyes turned on Isobel. "Hold it," she said. "I don't know. I would be in the way of you all. I can go visit my friends in UK. I still have family there."

Both Abby and Mary turned on her. "Of course you won't be in the way! You are part of the family now. We are all in your home being looked after, spoiled even. We would miss you if you went off now."

Isobel looked at Donny and John. Both smiled and shrugged.

"Well, I suppose you really need someone who knows how to sail a boat. I'll come and give you a few lessons."

She was still laughing as she fell back on the settee under a shower of cushions, thrown by her new 'family'.

Swallow nodded gracefully in response to the rows of small waves being driven down the coast of the Netherlands to the West. They were idling just north of Zandfoort as the big **DFDS** ferry to Amsterdam negotiated the entry into the river at Ijmuiden.

Isobel was at the helm, thoroughly content to be where she was with the company of the four people elsewhere on the boat. The ache of loneliness she had borne since the death of her husband and children would never entirely disappear, of that she was quite aware. But the presence of the three young people, and John, who was hardly old, had been a revelation. She felt that she belonged once more. She kicked the wheel, causing the sail to flutter and the boat to jerk. "Hey, below! I feel the need for relief."

A head appeared at the hatch, followed by a hand holding a glass of chilled white wine. Donny swung around and passed the glass on to Isobel, who received it gratefully. "I will forgive you, young man, if you can provide food for the starving crew."

The head disappeared, only to be replaced by Mary's. She grinned and lifted a plate of spring rolls, steaming still, and passed them over. "Starters! Stew and rice follows in five minutes." she disappeared.

Isobel sat back and tucked into the spring rolls with healthy appetite, contented once more.

There were white caps on the waves as the *Swallow* met the waters of the Kieler Bucht. All were on deck handling the sails that were now set for the voyage out into the Baltic proper, along the north coast of Germany en route for Riga, and Tallin, in Estonia,

The group had been together on the boat for eight days now and they had shaken down into a regular routine. John and Mary had confirmed the understanding that had really begun in the container on the way to France. Isobel was just part of the group, and often the arbiter in disputes over what to have for lunch, or even dinner.

Chapter Ten

It was the following day when trouble appeared. It came with a rush. John was the first to notice the speeding boat off to the south, between the ketch and the German shore.

The cabin cruiser was smart and fast, with a cabin designed for the luxury trade. About forty foot, it gained on the *Swallow* rapidly. John called out a warning to the others. Donny looked at the boat through the starboard porthole and reached out to the gun locker. As it dropped open Abby collected an H&K smg and slotted in the magazine. The armory had been enhanced in view of the increased crew. Two mini guns had been added and an extra Walther PPK in case of need. Isobel collected one mini gun and passed the other to Donny.

The cruiser quickly drew close to the ketch, and a figure appeared on deck clad in Hawaiian shirt and swimming shorts. He waved to Abby who lay on deck in her bikini, her gun out of sight beside her.

She waved lazily back at the man as the cruiser raced past. Below, Mary Tang unwrapped the hunting rifle. Her father had given it to her as a present on her twenty-third birthday. She had used it once; it was a Winchester Special, 30.06 caliber, firing a .22 bullet. The one occasion had been when she had sighted in the laser-scope shortly after receiving it. It was capable of delivering a bullet accurately over three-quarters of a mile. Because the steel-jacketed bullet had been found to fly through most animals without necessarily stopping them, the bullets were ceramic nosed, designed to shatter for maximum impact.

The magazine held seven shots in a clip, and there were ten clips in the accompanying box.

The cruiser had passed ahead of the *Swallow*, but now it turned in a wide sweep to pass the ketch once more. A man came on deck and joined the Hawaiian-shirted man. He carried a long narrow object, immediately identified by Isobel as a missile launcher.

Mary came on deck, heard what Isobel said, and returned below to collect her rifle. On deck, she loaded a clip and chambered a round.

On the cruiser the launcher was raised as the man lined up his shot. Mary raised the rifle to her shoulder and took rough aim before switching on the sight. Because of the movements of their respective boats neither of the shooters had an easy task. Mary had been taught to shoot birds on the wing with a .22 rifle from a child.

The gun was still weaving about with the motion of the boat when she fired.

For a moment nothing happened. Isobel thought she had missed. Mary lowered the rifle.

Aboard the cruiser, the man with the missile launcher looked down at his chest with amazement. His companion started to turn to see what was wrong. He was too late to stop his companion from dropping over the side of the cruiser, still gripping the launcher. He shouted to the helmsman, who turned the boat sharply away. The party on the ketch watched the cruiser disappear toward the coast at high speed. John Ling looked at Mary with respect. "Is there anything else you would like to tell me about before we set up home together?"

Mary looked at him startled. "You did not mention setting up house together."

"Who do you think I am? I did say I would stay with you. I am a man of my word. I assumed you also would keep yours to me." He looked at her quizzically.

"I...I...You..beast..... I. Of course I will." She stood looking lost, not knowing whether to laugh or cry.

Taking pity on her, John stepped forward and took her in his arms and kissed her. "I am learning new things about you every day. It looks like our life is going to be interesting."

The others all crowded round to congratulate the pair, and the tension of the moment was eased.

Meanwhile the cruiser disappeared over the horizon.

"Well, that's the end of the holiday. They now know where we are now and we have limited choices whilst we stay with the boat. I suggest we consider an alternative strategy." Donny paused and looked around at the others gathered about the cockpit of the boat. "What do you think of a showdown?"

"A showdown? What did you have in mind?" John Ling asked.

"How about us choosing our own ground. Then inviting them to come and get you."

He held up his hands to stop the babble of voices that greeted this suggestion. When he got silence again, he explained.

"We choose the battlefield. We are, or can be, well armed. Jonathon has told us that this man has limited time and resources at his disposal. It is only a matter of time. If we can hurt him enough, he will have to return to China empty handed."

"Sounds good. Any ideas where, when and how we go about this?" Isobel was cautiously optimistic.

"One suggestion: make for port and lose ourselves. Then, when we are ready, permit them to find us. Let the battle commence."

The others all expressed their agreement with this suggestion and their course was changed for Karlskrona in Sweden, taking them north but passing within easy reach of Bornholm, just in case they needed to leave the boat sooner.

In fact, the one hundred mile journey took them just twelve hours and they reached Sweden the following morning.

The party scattered, agreeing to rendezvous on the beach at Erguy, almost within sight of the Channel isles, to the west of St Malo.

Wu Fat looked at the bland face of Chen Li, seated opposite over the conference table. The voice of the Ambassador droned on. His dissertation was interrupted by the delivery of a message by hand of an aide.

"Gentlemen!" He spoke sharply and the entire table jerked to attention. "I have here a message from Beijing about the current operation in the matter of John Ling. If the matter cannot be resolved within the next five days, all resources will be withdrawn and Chen Li and his team will return to China immediately. The control of SDA assets in France remains the sole charge of Wu Fat. All reports of the operation will be channelled through Wu Fat and the correct chain of command. Any attempt to breach this order will be regarded as disobedience."

A chill came over the room at the wording of the message. Chen Li stiffened and looked at Wu Fat with hate-filled eyes. No word was said but the entire group knew that Chen Li faced censure when he returned home, unless he produced John Ling within five days and defamed him at the same time.

Wu Fat ignored the venomous look Chen Li gave him. Then, "How is your search going? Are we about to hear of a capture?"

"I will advise you when there is some positive news." The ungracious reply was noted and brought admonition that was unexpected from the normally, mildly spoken Wu Fat.

"There will be a report on your progress to date and a list of recommendations on my desk without fail by 2.00 pm. Is that understood?" The steely tone was out of character for Wu Fat.

Chen Li bowed his head. "It will be done," he said through clenched teeth.

The meeting broke up with the atmosphere still tense, with resentment and bitterness on the part of Chen Li and his followers.

In his own office Wu Fat sat down with a sigh. He thought for a few moments then sent for his chief aide.

David To was a trendy, well-dressed thirty-six year old. His life style was not reflected by his income. He spent and gambled at a level that had brought him to the attention of Wu Fat in the past. He had been kept under regular observation since.

Standing in front of his boss he was not quite as self-assured as he normally was. On this occasion, the old man had not invited him to sit. This was not a good sign.

Wu Fat studied his assistant for several seconds, noticing the appearance of the thin sheen of sweat that glistened on his deputy's forehead.

"When did you decide to start passing information out of this office?"

"Sir, information! Not me, sir. It must be another if any information had been leaked."

"Telling lies will not help your case." He held up his hand to stop further protests from the man. "You have been passing information to Chen Li ever since John Ling was released. Before I do anything about this I would like your own comment on how I should handle it. I confess my first thought was to send you home with a recommendation for further instruction in security procedure, and possible transfer to the Tibet administration in Lhasa. What do you think?"

"Sir, I beg you do not do that. I will do anything I can to regain your trust. I confess I was tempted to betray you, but it was minor information only, nothing serious. Mr Chen had information on me that he threatened to pass on to my parents. It would have hurt them terribly, so I accepted his money but gave very little in return."

"I have known of your particular liking for men for some time. Despite the effort you make to chat up the women in the Embassy, most of them are aware that you are harmless. I have never thought it necessary to make an issue out of it as long as you did your work efficiently. So now we have got that out of the way, to work once more. Explain what Mr Chen has demanded of you?"

"He was always asking for news of you and your family, especially your brother-in-law Robert Tang. He was under the impression that their daughter, Mary, was John Ling's partner who helped him escape from Le Havre when he first arrived here. There seems to be animosity toward you specifically. This I do not understand?"

"Chen Li came second in our studies at Shanghai University. He also failed to overtake me in training for the service we both chose. Finally, I was appointed to the Paris Embassy, the most prestigious posting in our diplomatic service. For these things I am never to be forgiven. Only when I have joined John Ling in the gutter, defamed and disgraced, will he be satisfied. Do you understand? So, now you choose sides. I will not ever tell your parents your secret, regardless of how you choose."

For the first time in his adult life David To felt completely humbled. He had always admired his superior, and having been trapped into serving Chen Li, had felt shamed by his betrayal, though helpless to do anything about it. His chief was actually giving him a chance to put things right. "How may I serve you, sir."

"I will explain..."

Jonathon Glynn put the telephone down, a small smile on his face. It disappeared as he realised what his friend Michael Weston, Donny's father, would say if he knew what Jonathon had just set up. He shrugged. Maybe he would not have to explain anything. He could get killed in the battle. After all people did die in battle, all the time, He shivered. Someone walked over his grave. Collecting his emergency case containing weapons and two changes of clothing, he rang the switchboard, told them he was away for the week, and set off for Petit Trecelin, the location of the house selected for the battleground.

The orchard extended towards the sea shore. The serried rows of fruit trees were heavy with apples at this time of year. The house stood at the top of the rise with all around views.

The friends gathered over a two day period.

The last to appear was Jonathon who had arranged the rental of the house. The owners had been happy to oblige Jonathon since the house was due for demolition, and had been off the holiday rental market for two years while the planning and the finance were being put into place. The early 19th century structure was still furnished and, to the current occupants, a place of antique charm, which should not have merited its imminent demise. The Parisian owners of the property had different ideas and no compunction at the destruction of this piece of history.

Located as it was in the north of Brittany, the apple orchards of the region surrounded the building. This provided cover for any attackers but the elevated position gave any defenders the advantage of a higher view point. From the attic rooms it was possible to spot intruders from over a mile in all directions. In the distance to the east, could be seen the sea.

The relationship between John and Mary had changed subtly. The warmth between them was clearly to be seen, and felt, by the others.

Isobel had taken over the kitchen. The big woodstove had over the past two days completely dissipated the last of the cold, unlived-in feeling of the house, felt by Donny and Abby when they had first arrived. They had flung open windows and lit fires in every fireplace to start the process, but it was the delicious scent of cooking food that finished the transformation. Perhaps for the last time, the house had come back to life.

In Paris. David To was beginning to understand the meaning of pain and the price of redemption. Chen Li did not normally regard himself as an impatient person. His problem at the moment was that time was against him. Either the problem was solved before the end of the week, or his return to China would be the first step on the path to complete political oblivion.

It was not a prospect he welcomed, so it was necessary to rush the extraction of information from

David To. This made it risky indeed. The main problem was that his subject was aware of the deadline, thus was aiming to last out until it was too late for Chen Li to take action to find and kill John Cheng and Mary Tang. Already two days of the five had passed and David To was still not giving his interrogators anything useful.

Chen regretted the fact that the real expert interrogators were all back in Beijing. They would have undoubtedly have extracted the necessary facts he needed to dispose of this task. It was still difficult for him to understand why such a simple operation could go wrong in the first place. He had put all the pieces in place to start with. Even the placement of Mary Tang had been pre-arranged. It was puzzling. Her profile had clearly shown that she would carry out the instructions to the letter. What had changed her mind?

It was possibly the weakness of Chen Li's preparations. He had not allowed for the possibility of love interfering, nor did he give sufficient credit to John Ling, whose intelligence had been severely under-rated, as had that of Mary Tang. It was the combination of the two challenged minds that had kept them free at the start, and it seemed their association with the English people had kept them safe up to now.

As he sat contemplating the possibility of failure, the news he had waited for came. David To had been broken. The entire party of the two fugitives and the three English had gone to a place called Petit Trecelin, near Erguy in Brittany. They were staying at a rented house on an apple-growing farm five kilometres from the village. David To swore he did not know the name of the house.

Chen Li gave immediate orders to go there, The team had been pre-selected and transport arranged. They left the battered figure of David To to the tender mercies of one of Chen Li's China forces. However, as soon as Wu Fat realised Chen was leaving, he stepped in and took over control of the tortured man. The man left by Chen tripped and fell down the stairs onto the stone flags of the cellar floor. He never recovered consciousness, and died that same day.

Chen's party was well on their way when his man died, and to tell the truth he would not have been troubled by the death, provided the man had divulged nothing incriminating on his final journey there.

The Paris traffic was horrendous as usual and the party in two Peugeot people carriers—Chen plus eight men and one woman—became thoroughly irritated in the process of getting out of Paris. It was dark by the time the raiding party was clear. A multiple pile-up on the ring road made a long diversion necessary.

They arrived at St Malo at 2:00 am, thoroughly irritated and tired from the long and wearisome trip that should have taken much less time. The cumulative effect of the trip and the sheer discomfort of travelling in a state of continuous stress caused by the obvious fury of their leader, made any thought of instant strike out of the question.

Thankfully, the party checked into a local hotel where they were able to rest until the next evening.

Meanwhile at the house the ambush was being prepared. Wu Fat had informed them that Chen Li had left with his entire entourage, heading for Normandy. The message had reached Jonathon as he was leaving Paris. It had reassured him that the scheme he had discussed with Donny was working. The Chinese would make the attempt to take John Ling. Wu Fat also promised to keep them posted on the progress of Chen Li's party. The beacon attached to one of the people carriers was working well.

At the house Jonathon, having greeted the friends, said, "I have brought one or two essentials in addition to the ammunition." He opened the trunk of his car and hauled out a long box. Inside were several small blocks of Semtex. A separate tin revealed impact fuses. He gave instructions on the fitting of the fuses to the Semtex. He and Isobel then located them in a semi-circle around the side of the house away from the drive. Having placed them, they armed each one individually, running a thin wire from one to the other, so that they could be all detonated together if required.

The trunk also contained a .303 Lee Enfield rifle with scope which was given to Abby. Her skill with a rifle had been tested, and proved.

At the front of the house he placed two tubes welded to base-plates, similar to mortars. He explained that they were grenade launchers. He demonstrated with a dummy grenade how to remove the pin and drop the grenade down the tube. "A jet of compressed air shoots the grenade out, the handle flies off and the grenade continues its flight to give the enemy a headache. I did try for the hand launchers, but these are more convenient. If all else fails, the grenades can be thrown in the traditional way." He grinned and hauled out a box of grenades and a box of mixed ammunition for the various weapons carried by the group.

For Donny and John the task was made easy by the cover provided by the rows of fruit trees. Normally well pruned by the time the fruit appeared, the foliage had thickened and a certain amount of extra growth had bushed the trees. In this case the orchard surrounding the house had been neglected for the past three years. The owners having died without surviving children, the consequent bickering over the inheritance had meant that no real work had been undertaken because of the expense involved. Thus far the only beneficiaries in the matter were the lawyers. The result was that the ground cover had grown unchecked. The usually clear straight avenues between the rows of fruit trees were in many cases becoming choked with bushes and uncut grass, providing cover for the two watchers stationed to give warning of the approach of the Chinese party led by Chen Li.

A call from Wu advised Jonathon that the opposition vehicles had been delayed in the pile-up on the Paris ring road. They were at least five hours behind. Jonathon had been able to avoid the accident, having been warned as he left the office and taken an alternate route.

He called to the watchers to come in, and when Donny and John came back to the house, he let Abby loose to sight-in her rifle. She actually fired twenty shots, with minute adjustments between each pair. Finally satisfied, she laid the rifle carefully on the mattress, confident she could hit a target up to 400 yards at least.

The whole group settled down to eat and relax, confident, at least for the next hour or so that there would be little chance of interruption.

The call that came at 2.30 am reported that the vehicles had stopped in St Malo.

The caller promised to advise them if the vehicles moved. Mary, who was on watch, took the message and carried on without waking the others. She passed the message on to Isobel when she took over at 4:00 am, allowing the others to sleep undisturbed.

Chapter Eleven

For Chen Li, time was pressing. The deadline he faced was causing him to make decisions in
haste and this was something that he had previously
avoided. Such decisions led to uncertain outcomes
and above all he preferred certainty. While his men
slept he rested with Pamela Chan. The sole female
member of his party was probably his most feared
agent. Born in Hong Kong her beauty had attracted
the attention of a Triad leader, who, though old, still
appreciated her extraordinary looks, young as she
was. His interest prevented her induction into the
training and lifestyle of the prostitute. Her protected
status allowed her natural abilities to be recognized
and the training in martial arts and the sensitive introduction to sexual practices made her rise in the
Triad ranks, even after the death of her sponsor.

She had come to Chen's notice when he was in
the security service. At that time he was involved in
undermining the establishment in Hong Kong, prior
to the handover from the United Kingdom.

Still a teenager at that time, Pamela was already
regarded with grudging respect within the criminal

fraternity. Chen was involved in working with the Triads at the time, a young ambitious operator with a future. Their mutual attraction led to an unprecedented deal with the Triad for her freedom. They had been together since that time.

Aware of his restlessness she turned to him. Kissing him softly she whispered, "Shall we make love? It may ease the hours of waiting." Her hand caressed his cheek.

"Tonight I can only think of our task. After we succeed we can relax properly. Until then, sleep and prepare."

He finally fell asleep. Pamela Chan slipped out of the bed and dressed silently. Taking her weapons required the very careful opening of the case at the foot of the bed. Her selection was limited by the need for silence. So she contented herself with a bandolier of six throwing-stars, and a Walther PPK automatic.

The people carrier started at the first turn of the key, the noise just part of the growing sounds of the wakening city.

At Matignon, she parked the vehicle and set off on foot to the now open, scooter-hire garage where she hired a scooter for the day. The area map, part of the hire package, showed the estates in the area and she was easily able to locate the target house.

Donny was also restless. Despite his certainty that they were doing the right thing, he was still worried about the danger to the three women, and still, it has to be said, wondering how they had reached this situation.

The entire affair had just seemed to transpire. He thought briefly about the word 'transpire', decided he liked it, just a little unsure if it fitted, but he liked it anyway.

He got up and slipped on his anorak. The light was bright from the rising sun but there was a cool nip in the air and a mist over the trees. He slipped the Glock into his holster in the small of his back and shrugged the jacket down to cover it. Then went out across the veranda and started to run. He chose a square pattern taking him up to the main road, then parallel to it for perhaps one kilometre before turning back down the row of trees to a final right angle back to the house.

He heard the scooter while he was running behind the hedgerow beside the road. He slowed, then stopped. The engine on the scooter stopped and the machine glided to a halt. The rider dismounted and wheeled the scooter into the cover of the thick hedge separating the estate from the road.

Donny crouched, peering through the hedge as the rider took off the helmet and shook her shining black hair out. It was short and neatly cut and it settled back in place demonstrating the skill of her hairdresser. She turned and Donny blinked. She was beautiful, and Chinese.

Well, well! Thought Donny. *What are the odds of a Chinese girl appearing at the roadside beside the estate where we are waiting for a visit from a bunch of Chinese?* He noted that she touched her back at belt level and unzipped her leather jacket. There was a flash of silver as she adjusted a belt under her jacket.

Weapons! Donny thought, and he continued to watch as she trotted off along the road to the nearby entrance to the estate. He saw her again as she came through the entrance and immediately took shelter under the first row of trees. The mist was clearing and the house was visible at the top of the long slope, the rows of trees leading the eye up the hill. They would provide concealment all the way up to the house, or at least to within twenty meters of the house.

The woman started off along the row of trees toward the house, making sure she was in cover as she went. Donny followed in a parallel row, keeping up with her but also making sure she did not see him.

She saw him, or thought she did and her reaction was swift and instinctive. The star appeared in her hand and was on its way without conscious thought. It disappeared and there was no reaction that she could see. Half-convinced that she had been mistaken she went to retrieve the razor-sharp throwing star.

Donny lay, gun in hand. The star had ripped his shoulder, tearing the jacket across the shoulder pad before dropping to the ground. The bleeding was inside the jacket so far. He had dropped and remained still as soon as he saw her move. It had saved him from more serious injury. On the ground he picked up the lethal star-shaped weapon and wiped the thin trace of blood off on his shirt. He tossed it carefully to the other side of the bushes which hid him, and with gun ready, he waited.

Pamela Chan came warily through the under-growth; the trees and bushes concealed her from the house, but instinct dictated caution. She saw the glint of the star on the ground, as she reached down for it there came a crashing in the bushes on her right. She picked up the star and swung round toward the noise. A wild boar came into view, mean little eyes fixed on her. They looked at each other for some seconds, then, as if by mutual consent, each turned away and went off in the other direction.

Donny sighed, uncocked the Walther and winced as he moved his wounded shoulder. He care-fully lifted back his jacket to expose the wound. The thin red cut was a line across the top, not deep but it was now painful. He had been lucky. An inch lower it would have hit solidly and caused a lot more dam-age, not the least, by probably giving his presence away.

The wild boar had been an unexpected bonus, taking her mind off the search at a critical time.

He may have been able to shoot her before she finished him, but it was a big question mark. She was fast!

He took his cell phone from his pocket. It was set on silent mode. He texted Jonathon.

"We have a visitor. I am in the orchard approx 40 ms below the lounge window. Visitor is between me and you. She is very lethal." He clicked send and waited, gun ready once more.

From the house came the sound of fierce dogs barking. Donny looked up in astonishment. He knew there were no dogs in the house so what was going on?

The rustle of disturbed bushes over to his left gave the answer. The visitor was taking no chances. The sound retreated toward the road. The sound of the scooter starting up followed.

In the house Donny was being thoroughly berated by Abby while Isobel cleaned his wound and brought the lips of the cut together with a broad plaster.

Donny moved his arm experimentally, finding that it was quite mobile despite the pain when he accidently pulled it.

Jonathon said, "She was obviously an advance scout for the opposition. Probably left her car in the village and hired the scooter for the last part of the trip. Tonight, I think. That's my guess. They'll attack tonight."

The others were silent. Isobel had gone back to the kitchen and was preparing lunch. Abby and Mary were sitting, listening. John was roaming the grounds keeping an eye out for visitors.

Pamela Chan reached the Hotel in St Malo in just over an hour after leaving the house near Petit Trecelin.

Chen Li was not happy but he was pleased to hear the news about the location of the house and the general layout of the area around it. The cover described by Pamela Chan would make it easier to approach undetected. He was not so happy about the calibre of the men he had here to work with. None of them was up to the standard of Pamela Chan. Had there been more time to assemble his team he would have drawn in people from other parts of China. As it was he had to make do with what he had. At least they were all willing, and they were all Chinese. The mercenaries he had worked with so far had all been unreliable.

He planned to start the assault at dusk. With the uncertain light at that time it would cover the approach up through the avenues of trees leading to the house.

Donny watched the light fade with growing apprehension. He wasn't scared, but there was a lot riding on their success tonight. He had no illusions. Jonathon had made it quite clear that Chen Li would not be happy to return to China without a successful outcome. The chances were that if he failed, his career was likely to be short and terminal. His sponsors did not do failure. Thus far Chen Li had done well, until his last task which had been only partially successful. He was now on trial, and having set out on this task with every confidence, it had suddenly gone wrong. Each and every action he had taken to put things right, had misfired. He blamed the help, but his masters would not be impressed by excuses.

Donny sighed. When someone who had proved himself that ruthless had his back to the wall, all hell was likely to break loose. He shrugged, and was sharply reminded that at least one of Chen Li's people was good, very good. He eased his shoulder under his flak jacket, and checked the magazine of his smg. Well, they had baited the trap and laid the ambush. Now they waited.

He started as a hand touched his shoulder. Abby whispered, "It's spooky, isn't it."

"It certainly is. The trouble is always the waiting. Once things get going, it's fine. It's just the waiting." As he stopped, the radio beside him clicked once.

"Right, everyone. Our visitors have arrived." Donny stood and stretched. "John will be on his way in. Careful you don't shoot him by mistake."

"Anyone who does will have to answer to me," the voice of Mary came from the next room.

"Quiet, everyone!" Jonathon ordered from the back room. "I can hear you all from here."

Standing beside the front door Donny waited for John. The radio clicked twice, Donny opened the door and let John in. "The signals worked anyway. But no more talking. I could hear you all halfway down the field."

Mary slid up to him and hugged him. "Like something to eat or drink?"

"Not just now. Perhaps later," John replied. "Now back to your place," He smacked her lightly on the bottom and shooed her off. Settling down to wait with Donny beside the front door, he said quietly, "About thirty minutes."

"Will you be going back to China? After all this I mean." Donny's voice was low, just enough to reach John.

There was a pause while John thought about it. Then "I really don't know. Possibly not. I did not anticipate Mary, and I am tired of looking over my shoulder all the time. It would be nice to relax and live a normal life for a change, without people depending on me all the time."

He paused thinking, then.. "I have been on the run for three years, then prison for two." He smiled shyly. "Until Mary, I have never made love. Oh, I've had sex," he said hastily. "But I have never had a romance prior to that terrible trip in the container."

Donny looked at his companion in the dim light. "You and she are really committed then?"

"Yes. I hope when this is all over, we will marry and settle either here or in Britain or the USA."

As Donny went to speak again, John held up his hand. The faint noise and flash of a firecracker came from the lower end of the orchard.

"They are about thirty meters from the road." He said quietly, "I left a few trip-wires to liven things up."

"I'll be back." Donny left John to go upstairs to Abby, where she lay waiting beside the mounted rifle at the upstairs room window.

Mary, who had been talking quietly with Abby, disappeared downstairs when Donny arrived. "All set?" he asked as he lay down beside Abby.

She gathered him in her arms, "Be careful, please. I have a long and happy future mapped out for us and I do not want it spoiled by a bunch of Chinese gunmen."

Donny kissed her and held her close. "I have an interest of my own in this deal. I would just like to point out that you are important to me, and that we could have sailed away after the first contact in Boulogne. He quickly kissed her once more and reluctantly released her, standing up to return downstairs. "Not long now, they are in the orchard." As he turned to go he said, "We'll try the Azores next, perhaps take John and Mary with us. See you later." And he was gone.

Mary returned. "I think he wants to marry me," she said.

"And what do you think?" Abby asked, her eyes concentrating on the orchard in the deepening dusk. She lifted the rifle to her shoulder and peered down the sight. The night scope lit the view in a green glow and she could see the two men who had crawled up to the edge of the trees twenty metres away. She breathed out and relaxed squeezing the trigger gently. The thud of the silenced rifle shot was followed immediately by a second thud as the second man dropped beside his shot partner. The bolt of the rifle was smooth and clicked easily as it slid back into place with another bullet loaded in the breech and ready to fire. Both shot bodies were now lying still, dead or unconscious. Abby scanned the area in front of her for any movement.

Pamela Chan had some comments to make about the quality of the men that had accompanied her to the Orchard estate. Chen Li was in the people carrier waiting for the report from the attacking party. He had retained one man as insurance. Pamela had set out with seven men. She now knew that two were gone, probably killed. Her report to Chen Li merely said that the two were out of touch. The others were all under her direct control. She spread the men out over a fifty-meter front, to approach the house in a line. She was behind the middle man when he blew-up. Actually, he did not blow-up. It was the ground beneath his feet that blew up. The effect was the same, as the man lost all interest in the project.

Though not killed, he was completely out of it for the next hour at least, that is, if he ever recovered.

Pamela shrugged. *Rather you than me,* she thought and crossed the line of charges stepping over the recumbent figure, whose jeans were smoking, singed at the ankle.

She spoke to the surviving men over her radio, "Close up to the house and wait!"

She moved to the edge of the clearing and looked up at the dark building. As she ducked and slid behind a tree, a bullet caught her sleeve, scoring the leather of her jacket without making a hole. She felt the groove with her right hand, cursing under her breath. The designer jacket had cost her a lot of money. Then she chuckled under her breath, "Who goes on a killing mission in the dark, to a strange country area, in designer leather? Answer, an idiot."

She felt better for a moment then realized that the shooter must have a silenced rifle and a night-scope, at least. In addition unless it had been a lucky shot, the sniper was good. She did not think it was luck.

In the house, Abby said "Bugger, missed him."

Mary said, "I think you may have clipped him, but perhaps not. There seems to be no reaction and certainly he must be behind a tree or something. He has disappeared completely."

Mary had been watching through a spare night-scope. She commented "I think it might be a woman."

"What makes you say that?" Abby had not really thought about that. Recalling the slender shape in the grainy green picture through the sight, she conceded it might indeed have been a woman.

Jonathon and John had stepped out to the tree line, settled down in cover and waited. With Donny at the other side of the house, they concentrated on the two men on their side.

It nearly cost them their lives. John heard the whisper of a movement. He had no time to warn Jonathon. He was looking directly at the two intruders as they came out of the shadows. They were more surprised than John. Neither managed to do more than start lifting their weapons before John fired, the silenced automatic bucking in his hand. Neither survived.

Donny spotted the two men on his side of the house, "Stop where you are, don't move!"

The urgency in his voice, following the explosion that had blown up their comrade, made an impact. Both men froze on the spot. "Guns down," Donny said. Both carefully grounded their weapons. Donny came forward and directed them carefully to the door of the house where the girls secured them. Donny contacted Jonathon, who reported the demise of the two men on that side of the house.

Using a radio taken from one of the dead men, John took the call from Pamela Chan.

Under the trees Pamela called her surviving men. One reply came, though not from her man. "Miss Chan, it might be in your interest to retire. Two of your men have survived. Both are visiting the house at the moment feeling relieved to be alive, I understand. Unless you wish to join them, I suggest a short de-brief with your boss, keeping your hand firmly on your weapon of choice. Then perhaps a vacation in the south while your boss explains why his plans went wrong to his Beijing masters. You may of course survive whatever happens, but your chances with the Chinese option could be questionable."

Pamela Chan thought for a moment. "Your sniper has me pegged at the moment. If I move, I will be in his sights."

"You are allowed to leave. I will see you to your vehicle safely—if it is still there, of course. Your leader has gained a reputation for not suffering failure happily."

As Pamela listened to the voice she tried to place it. Then it came to her that this was John Ling, the target of the operation. If he was going to accompany her to the road there might be an opportunity to take him with her, or kill him perhaps, on the way.

"Will it be you accompanying me to the road personally?"

"I did have that in mind."

"Then I accept your offer of escort."

"Please stand and remove your belt of throwing stars, just lay it on the ground. You may keep your gun. You may need it when you greet your boss. You will be in someone's sights all the way. We will take the main drive to the road, if you would care to lead the way?"

Pamela Chan stood up, and slipping off her jacket, removed the bandolier of throwing stars and placed them on the ground at her feet. She donned her jacket once more concealing the Walther in the waistband holster, thinking wryly that it would not be of too much use at the moment. She could not see her escort nor could she guess where he would appear from.

In fact he did not appear at all though he obviously was paralleling her progress down the main drive. She walked almost feeling the sniper following her in his sights as she walked along the exposed track to the road.

Chapter Twelve

Three days later Pamela Chan stood at the window of the apartment in Dijon looking at the street below. She wondered for the umpteenth time if she had made the right decision.

"We will dine out tonight." The voice from the bedroom interrupted her train of thought.

"Good, I am beginning to enjoy the cuisine of this area. Do I dress up? Or down?"

Chen Li walked through from the bedroom and joined her. He came over and slipped his arms round her from behind, holding her close and cupping her breasts in both of his hands.

"You are beautiful," he said softly. "We should have done this, years ago."

"But you have known me for years." She teased him, as she relaxed back against him, feeling his body respond to the contact. She took his hands away from her breasts and stepped forward. First I must go shopping. I will meet you for lunch at the restaurant. Where shall we go to eat?"

As she moved away from him she was aware that for a second he had almost held on and not let her go. There was still anger in him and she now realized there always would be. It would not have changed, even if they had managed to take John Ling. For Chen Li the world was out of step, not he. He hated the fools in Beijing. He hated Wu Fat. He hated John Ling, and she suspected that while he used her, he hated her as well.

The moment passed and he named a restaurant on the edge of the town centre. "At 12:30 pm then; I will see you there." She kissed him, picked up her bag and left the apartment. He watched her from the window. She looked pretty in her pale blue dress, with the navy jacket slung over her shoulders against the slight autumn chill. She was useful and skilled in bed as well as with the weapons she carried. It was convenient to have her as cover while things calmed down. Then, when he had let the matter settle—allowing them to think it was all over—he would strike swiftly and finally. Perhaps Pamela would be a part of the smear campaign, the scandal that would follow John Ling's death. She knew too much to be permitted to survive.

Pamela Chan was no fool. She went shopping, dropping in first at the Clemenceau Hotel to make a telephone call. At the Chinese Embassy Wu Fat picked up the phone. "Yes?" He said.

"I am Pamela Chan. I stay with Director Chen Li."

"Director Chen Li is no longer director, nor is he part of our embassy here."

"Wu Fat, don't talk. Listen! Chen Li intends to kill John Ling and anyone else who gets in his way. He thinks it will solve his problems if he does this and he will stop at nothing to do it. You, he hates anyway. If he gets the chance you will be killed as well. I am happy to retire here in France and stay out of politics but Chen is not under my control. Warn all people involved. I will try to warn you when he decides to make the attempt."

"What do you want Miss Chan? Why are you doing this?"

"I am not foolish enough to think he will spare me when he gets going. I know too much. I would like stay in France when it is all over and try a quiet, normal life, for a change. Can you arrange it?"

"If what you say, and do, comes true and we survive, it will be arranged."

"Thank you, Wu Fat." The phone shut off. There was no ring back when he requested it.

Wu Fat sat and thought for a while. Then he collected his cigarettes and with them in his hand left the building. He had taken up smoking at this late date because it gave him the perfect excuse to leave the building. He had realised the idea's effectiveness when he saw the number of people standing outside every public building, all smoking. The ban on smoking in government buildings was taking its toll on the efficiency of the public service in no uncertain terms.

Outside he was able to mingle with the others gathered there. No one showed any interest in him particularly. He had become faceless.

There was a public telephone round the corner on the busy main street and it was from there he was able to get in touch with Jonathon Glynn. He passed on the warning from Pamela Chan, without mentioning her name. Jonathon put two and two together and suggested that it was Pamela Chan and that he would welcome her retirement. He would be pleased to assist in her relocation when the time came.

Once the deadline had passed, the party in the Brittany house had gathered their things and returned to Paris. Jonathon preceded them, leaving the day after the abortive attack by Chen Li's men.

After a week back in Paris the party gathered in Isobel's apartment to plan their proposed trip to the Azores. The boat was still in Sweden so Donny and John agreed to fetch it to back to Amsterdam. There they would provision and be met by the three women. Isobel did suggest they would be better to go without her but they would not hear of it. So it was, in the absence of their men, the three women did what most women might do in the circumstances. They went shopping for suitable clothing for the forthcoming voyage.

"I'm not happy with the outcome of this business involving Chen Li. It's all too pat, too easy.

Every instinct is telling me that it is not all over yet."
Donny was not able to relax despite the soporific effect of the water under the keel of the 40 ft ketch.

John smiled. "*I feel by the pricking of my thumbs something wicked this way comes.*" You are shying at shadows I think. Remember the SAD had pulled the plug on Chen Li. He is powerless."

"Powerless but not helpless. That man showed all the signs of complete paranoia. He was obsessed with catching you and clearing his name with his backers. If, even now, he manages to blacken your name and/or get you back to Beijing involved in a scandal, he will be vindicated and re-established in his former position at least. Am I right?"

"Yes. I suppose so. But he has lost his followers except for, what was her name? Pamela Chan."

"As I recall," Donny said dryly, "Pamela Chan is worth three of most men! And he has funds."

"Okay. You've convinced me. So why has he not tried anything so far?"

"Oh. Come on, John. Put yourself in his position. You have to plan. Then you have to decide whether to jump in, in a hurry. Oops, that was tried. It didn't work well, so let's think. If we wait until everyone has settled down, perhaps they will be off guard and things will be simpler."

John nodded in agreement. "I see what you mean. So we would be better well away before he gets things together?"

"Preferably!"

"Now you have me worried, with the girls all at home alone."

"I would hesitate to tackle Isobel or Abby, and come to think of it, Mary seems quite at home with a gun in her hand." Donny was sounding more confident that he felt. "Anyway we'll be in Amsterdam tomorrow morning. So why don't you ring Mary just now. You can pass on our thoughts about Chen Li at the same time."

John went below to make the call while Donny sat back at the wheel trying not to let the niggle of worry spoil his day.

"They are on the train to Amsterdam now. No signs of anyone following, but they are all wary of strangers. Mary knows Chen Li, but any oriental is suspect at present. So they are all on guard."

Donny was relieved though he merely nodded in acknowledgement.

Neither of them had much to say for the next two hours. Both were thinking of possible ways they could be vulnerable to attack by Chen and his sole surviving aide, Pamela Chan.

The express drew smoothly into Amsterdam Central station and the three women prepared to venture forth into the busy city. The sky was blue with patchy clouds, the sun was out but it was cooler than Paris. Because the baggage had been enhanced in Paris they needed the cab to take them to their hotel.

Despite the precautions they had taken in Paris they had been observed while boarding the train to Amsterdam. The private investigator hired by Chen Li did not know whether they were booked all the way to Amsterdam or perhaps to one of the intervening stations on the way.

The Krasnapolsky Hotel is located in Dam Square, and the taxi journey from the Central Station was over very quickly. The smooth efficiency of the cheerful porters soon had them installed in the suite provided, at her insistence, by Isobel.

The arrival of Jonathon Glynn was a surprise. He was accompanied by a serious, mature-looking man dressed in an expensive but untidy tweed sports jacket, chequered shirt and a club tie. The picture was completed by the brown hair that, by the look of it, had been forgotten and was finger-combed at the last minute.

He was introduced by Jonathon as Adam Brown, on temporary attachment to MI6. He did not elaborate but he did say, "Ladies, I am aware of your talents. You have all demonstrated your abilities in looking after yourselves in the difficult circumstances of the past few weeks."

He looked at the three attentive faces in front of him. Then "I have to warn you that Chen Li has been recruiting. I have been informed that he has recruited a team of ex-Spetsnaz to assist in some unspecified operation. My informant and I agree that you all, as a group, are the target. So, apart from my personal reluctance to throw you to the wolves, I understand that you still do not wish to come into protective custody as my boss suggests. So I have brought along a friend, just to even the odds a little. Adam is familiar with just about any form of mayhem you can imagine, and more important, has worked with, and against, the Spetsnaz on several occasions."

He paused and held up his hand to quiet the burst of questions from his audience. He looked at Abby.

"Your parents have no idea what you are currently doing. So far, I have not told them and I won't, provided you accept Adam into the team. I'm aware the accommodation on the *Swallow* will be a little cramped, but this is not negotiable. If Adam goes you all go. Without him nobody goes!"

The knock on the door announced the return of Adam Brown complete with a big tote bag slung over his shoulder.

"I'll doss down in the lounge here if that is okay with you ladies." He had a quiet voice with the faint tinge of London in the accent. "I'll try not to get in your way too much." He was beginning to feel a little uncomfortable in the silence that had greeted his suggestion.

Abby regarded him critically for a few moments."Sit down!" she said in a clear clipped voice that did not allow for argument.

"Now I....We want to know just who the hell you are and why does Jonathon think we need you to look after us?"

Having sat in an armchair with the three ladies on the settee opposite he told them.

"I am Adam Brown, a Royal Marine for the past fifteen years, seven of which were in the Special Boat Service. I am on terminal leave. I have worked on occasion for MI5 and 6, during my service. I have been offered a place in MI6 when I retire, but I won't be taking it." At this point he stopped.

Isobel said, "How old are you Adam?"

"I'm thirty-five!" He said surprised.

"Married?" This from Mary.

"Was once. She left me for a banker; decided she was too much on her own. I was pretty upset at the time, but I guess I understand now."

Abby said "Why are you leaving? Why are you here?"

Adam smiled wryly. "I had reached the point where I was faced with promotion and a Commission. That meant leaving the SBS and returning to a regular Marine Unit. For me personally, that would not be possible. I could not stay on as a Sergeant. So I resigned.

"Your second question is easy. Two reasons: MI6 pays well and going into the big wide world after the Marines costs money. The other is that I was told your story, and knowing the Russians are involved, thought I could help, and at the same time honor a debt. Two of them tortured and killed some friends of mine in Afghanistan."

The room was silent. Then Mary said, "While we are here we have to do something about the clothes."

Isobel added, "And the hair."

"Hey! What's up with my clothes, hair? Hey! That's my gear." He spoke too late to prevent his bag being upended onto the carpet. The collection of creased and crumpled clothes, the box of loaded magazine for a Beretta 9mm automatic, soap bag and toiletries looked sort of forlorn in the rich surroundings of the suite. He started to collect his things and stuff them back in the bag.

Isobel spoke up, "Adam, look at us."

He straightened and looked at the three women, all casually dressed in designer clothes, each stunning in their own way."

"What?" He said puzzled.

"Look in the mirror, man!" As he looked at himself in the mirror the three women joined him. His heart sank as he looked. "I'll get some other gear," he said dejectedly.

"We will get some other gear, and before you say anything, this comes under expenses." Isobel was adamant. The other two joined in and that was that.

The hairdresser from the hotel was summoned to sort out the hair. After a certain amount of argument, the compromise was grudgingly accepted as okay by the disgruntled Adam.

While the hair was being dealt with, a selection of casual clothing and some suits were delivered. The resultant selection was approved by the ladies, now satisfied that Adam would not be out of place in their company.

To celebrate they lunched in the hotel where Adam decided to co-operate and managed to select the correct cutlery throughout the meal.

As he lay on the lounge settee that night he reflected that he was actually pleased with the result of the makeover. He had been letting the standards drop over the past few years since his wife had left him. He had lost it for a while when the divorce came through. It had been a real shock to find out that she actually had meant it and had gone forever. Luckily he had been detached to Afghanistan at the time and just surviving had been difficult enough. Alfie—his best friend, Alfred Walker from Bow, East London—had prevented him getting killed that first time. He had known more about dirty in-fighting that anyone else Adam had ever met, even among the instructors at Hereford, the home of the SAS. It didn't help when the bomb went off. Poor Alfie, stuck in a wheelchair now, but still telling the stories in his pub in Wapping.

The girls had taken him to a disco that evening and he found himself dancing among a crowd of others, to ear-splitting music that consisted mainly of beat with bugger all melody. The girls enjoyed it though, he thought with a smile, recalling the swaying bodies as he drifted off to sleep.

Jonathon called in and wished them bon voyage on his way back to Paris. He agreed to meet up again when they returned from the Azores. Promising invitations to the wedding next spring, he departed in a rush to catch his train.

The *Swallow* tied up at the marina the next day. All four of them went down to meet Donny and John at the pontoon where they were tied up. With introductions made the six people adjourned to the marina café which overlooked the moored boats. From the café Adam was able to pick out the *Swallow* where she lay alongside a pontoon between a big German boat, and a motor sailor of Dutch registration.

As the party relaxed over coffee and pastry, Adam kept his eye on the moored boat. He noticed the two men in jeans and sweaters walking backward and forwards up and down the pontoons progressing across the marina from the far end. It took a few moments for him to realize that they were looking for a particular boat.

"Excuse me!" He said interrupting Donny half-way through his description of the journey through the Kiel Canal. "We have company, I believe."

All five stopped what they were doing and looked out of the window across the moored boats. "If I am right, they will come to *Swallow* on the next leg of their walk."

As they watched the two men reached the boat and even from the café it was possible to see the re-action of the pair. Like a silent movie they saw the finder call to the other man who hurried over to look at the name on the counter of the boat. They held a discussion, then while one man went off out of the gate to the telephone box, the other settled down to wait. He seated himself at the far end of the pon-toon. Adam picked up the binoculars provided for the use of guests. Adjusting them he focussed on the seated man. "Well, well," he muttered. "Grigor has made it to the big time."

"What was that? You know the man?" Donny asked.

Chapter Thirteen

There was a sudden silence as the entire group waited for Adam's response.

"I certainly do. The last time I saw him I had just shot him. He and a couple of his friends had slotted two of our friendly Afghanis and I was lucky enough to turn up in time to get what I thought was one of the killers. Apparently the report of his death was exaggerated, or he had a twin brother." Adam wandered across towards the door deep in thought.

Donny nodded to John who had heard what Adam had been saying. They crossed to the door and met Adam there.

"What did you have in mind?" Donny asked.

"Well, my first thought was to finish what I started four years ago. My second thought was to re-connoitre the marina and find out where the cover man is situated so that I can neutralize him first."

"Then what?" John asked.

"Then remove Grigor; knowing that the sting would have been removed from the opposition's capability to hurt us." He looked at the others innocently. "After all, that is what I am here for. Isn't it?"

Donny couldn't help smiling at the question which did not in any way really cover the presence of Adam in their midst.

"Let us discuss this between us. I think it would be a good idea if we all knew what we were doing. After all, everyone here, including you, is valuable. We are a team, let's keep it that way. What do you say?"

Adam shrugged. "When you put it that way, what can I say? Let's get to it then."

They joined the others. All three women were curious at the little scene that had just been played out at the café door. Though the restaurant was nearly empty, there were still a few people showing interest in the group.

When the men rejoined the women, the onlookers lost interest in them and returned to their own affairs.

Mary said quietly, "That pair over there, near the door is still watching us. I seem to recognize the woman from somewhere." John used the moment of seating himself to take a quick look. The couple near the door had entered after the group, whilst they were getting settled down in their seats. Now, as he noticed them for the first time, John realised that the girl, who was brown haired, with her eyes concealed behind dark glasses, was familiar to him also. He seated himself trying to place the almost instinctive recognition of the woman, and realized that it was the body language that was familiar. Then he remembered the woman from the house with the throwing stars. "That is Pamela Chan, sitting with the man at the table near the door."

Adam looked up, having missed the earlier comment by Mary. He looked straight into the startled eyes of Grigor's back-up man. While the others looked on amazed, he drew his suppressed automatic, and, offhand, fired.

The small sound was lost in the chatter of the café conversations. The Russian had started to get up. He sat back in his seat with a sigh. His companion Pamela Chan froze in her place. There was nowhere for her to go, and she realized it.

Adam rose and nodded to Isobel who left her seat and joined him as he walked over to greet the couple like old friends. Pamela responded, lifting her hand into view to show the handcuff round her left wrist. The dead Russian was still sitting upright in his seat. There was a pump shotgun hanging down inside the back of his bulky overcoat, trapped between him and the chair. It had been enough to keep him erect in his seat. Adam and Isobel sat down at the table and Adam used the moment to start checking the pockets of the dead man.

The handcuff key was on the chain with others in his trouser pocket. Adam removed the cuffs from both of them. Pamela said, "Thank you, whoever you are." She turned to Isobel. I was trying to contact you, but that Russian bastard, Grigor, insisted I came as cover while he looked for your boat. As soon as we left Chen Li I was cuffed onto Yuri here. No explanation, so I reckon Chen Li has no more use for me. I warned Jonathon that he was coming for you."

Adam said, "Let's move on, shall we?"

Isobel called to the others and they all came over crowding around the table, greeting the seated couple. Then Adam and Donny, who was the taller ones, collected the Russian between them. Screened by the others, they left the restaurant in a chattering group taking Yuri, the Russian with them.

Grigor was no longer waiting and watching at the boat. A scan with Jonathon's bug detector quickly turned up two bugs located on the hull. The cabin lock was untouched but they checked the interior anyway.

The body could have been embarrassing but, since they were putting to sea, they decided he could wait until open water for a burial at sea. His body was wrapped in a plastic sheet purchased hastily from the chandlers shop by Abby while they removed all labels and tags from Yuri, ensuring there were no remaining identifying marks on his clothing. The shotgun was added to the armoury.

They sailed at 2:00 pm.

The simple ceremony was held offshore five sea miles north-west of Zandfoort. The body slid into the North Sea with hardly a ripple, still wrapped in its plastic shroud with a length of scrap chain, picked up outside the repair yard at Ijmuden, at the seaward end of the North Sea canal. Wound around and secured to his feet, it helped him sink.

Pamela Chan was still with the group making the boat more crowded than was comfortable. The discussion as to her future was conducted in her presence. It was she who had provided the solution to her problem. They were currently planning on a brief stop at Cherbourg for fresh milk and bread before departing for the mid-Atlantic islands. She would go ashore at Cherbourg and take her chances. She had her own resources. If she had not been trapped by the resurgence of Chen Li's plan to kill John Ling and Donny and Abby, she would have been already off on her own at her pre-selected retreat in the Massif Central.

It was convenient for the party to accept her story, the handcuffs and her apparent sincerity impressing them all. Donny retained some doubts but he allowed himself to be persuaded by the others.

For the two days sailing the rotation of watches meant that they could all have somewhere to sleep. With two on watch at all times there was always a spare berth.

By the time they arrived at Cherbourg all of them were feeling rather worn. A unanimous decision was reached to spend at least one night there before setting off once more. They checked in to the hotel as a party of seven; Pamela agreeing that she would leave when the others set off.

Donny had impressed on the others not to divulge the location, or even the existence of the locker where the weapons were kept.

When the party went ashore the personal weapons went with the group. Pamela was the only one not armed. She shared a room with Isobel. They all separated to their different rooms to get some well earned rest.

The following morning it was by accident that Donny found out that they had a Judas goat. He had decided to check and replace the battery in the bug detector. And having switched it on in the hotel room, he got a positive signal. It was strongest beside the wall between their room and the room shared by Isobel and Pamela.

He discussed it with Abby who suggested that it could have been planted on Pamela by Chen Li "She may not be aware of it. The thing is what do we do about it? It is probably already too late. Stopping it will merely give away the fact that we know."

They decided to keep the information to themselves and see what happened. As Donny put it, "I am tired of running, and this man seems obsessed."

Pamela, John and Mary were shopping with Adam in tow when the pick-up occurred. The Russians closed in around Pamela, John and Mary.

Adam was missed as he was looking at something away from the group. He recognized the men as they eased the three captives to the door. Adam followed, phoning Donny. At the same time Abby grabbed Isobel and gave her the news. Donny came into town with the other two and joined Adam who, without a car, had been trying to find a taxi.

"We need an electronics shop, a Radio Shack if possible."

Adam said, "I've seen a radio and TV repair place, will that do?"

He directed Donny to turn down a side street to a dingy looking shop with several tired-looking radio's and TV's in the window. There was also a scanner.

Donny dived through the door and spoke to the slim young man inside. "Have you a receiver that will pick up signals on this frequency." He reeled off the numbers from memory.

The youth looked at him warily. "That's not legal," he said.

Donny produced a bundle of euro notes. "Have you?"

At the sight of the notes the young man brightened up. From under the counter he produced a small instrument with an extending aerial. Donny took and tuned the control to the frequency. The beep, beep, of the signal came through quite clearly. "How much?" He said.

"Two hundred euros." The young man replied.

"Here!" Donny said, thrust some notes at the man turned and left the shop. In the car he said to Adam, "You drive. I'll navigate."

The signal was not difficult to follow and Adam began catching up to the crew car that was used by the Russians. "Are you all carrying?" Donny asked.

Isobel and Adam both nodded. Abby produced her Walther and checked the magazine and the safety catch before returning it to her waist band holster. "The pump gun is behind the back seat," Donny said. Isobel reached over and found it under the rug that had concealed it from prying eyes. She checked the indicator and confirmed that the gun was fully loaded.

The Russian's vehicle was actually in sight when it turned off the road down a country lane. Out of town the Normandy countryside was fields with patches of woodland scattered at intervals. Their quarry turned off onto another side road finally stopping at a large house within a small wood.

The Russians entered the house with their prisoners leaving one of the men outside as security. Adam drew up about four hundred meters from the house, pulling their vehicle into a gate entry to one of the fields, off the road itself.

Inside the house, the prisoners were taken into the downstairs drawing room. It was decorated like a scene from a BBC Victorian drama, tall windows with long drapes, currently closed. The heavy furniture was scattered around the crowded room with the floors highly polished in the area that was clear of the scatter rugs. John allowed himself to be pushed and was able to confirm that the polish extended under the rugs, making them liable to skate around if the chance came. As the party stood there, another door, disguised as part of the panelling, opened and Chen Li walked in.

Seeing John Ling, a smile crossed his face. He noted the presence of Pamela and his face hardened. Then seeing Mary, he nodded, satisfied that his orders had been followed. He spoke to the Russian, Grigor. "Arrange some coffee. This could take some time."

Grigor growled to one of his men in Russian. The man nodded and left the room. The three Russians stationed themselves around the room and Chen Li ordered the three prisoners to sit on the settee, side by side. Pamela and Mary seated either side of John.

John cautiously tried the carpet under his feet. Satisfied he sat back and waited for the proceedings to begin. He was hoping that Adam had seen what had happened and that help was on the way. The trouble was that he was not sure.

Chen Li spoke at length about the trouble caused by the interference of the English and their boat. He added that he would make arrangements for their punishment when he got back to China.

He spoke to John. "I am sure you will be happy to be back with your people in China once more. Though by then I do not think you will have many friends left."

He paused "I have decided that you will be shot in your home village. That should put to rest any further treason from that quarter.:

He then turned to the others. To Mary he said, "You will no doubt be pleased that I intend for you to die alongside your lover. You see I am a romantic at heart." To Pamela Chan he smiled sardonically. "For you, my dear, the reward of personal betrayal." He changed to Mandarin. "First, I have promised these Russian pigs your services for three days. On the fourth I will take pleasure in killing you slowly, inch by inch."

Chen rose to his feet and walked over to the seated figure and stood in front of her. "You have been useful to me despite your betrayal." He pulled Pamela's head forward and reached down the back of her blouse. He unsnapped her brassiere. Without bothering about the pain he was inflicting, he wrenched it up snapping the shoulder straps and twisting her breasts in the process. Her involuntary cry of pain was ignored.

Holding the brassiere up in front of the three seated prisoners he showed them the flat button-sized transmitter attached to the back strap of the undergarment. "We followed your progress all the way from Amsterdam," he said triumphantly.

The door opened and expecting the Russian with the coffee, it was ignored. All eyes were on the drama in front of them. The voice from the door jolted them back to reality.

"And we followed her all the way here." The words spoken in English galvanized the room occupants into action. John kicked the carpet under his feet causing Chen Li to stagger and his shot at John to go high. All three hit the floor, John once more unbalancing Chen Li, this time taking the legs from under him.

The room was filled with the crash of gunfire. Adam had selected Grigor and his first two shots put him down. Chen Li was on the floor, his gun out of reach. John Ling lay across his legs and Pamela Chan smashed her leg across his exposed throat, once, twice, then a third time to make sure. With a shudder Chen Li went limp. His chest heaved in an attempt to drag air into his lungs past his crushed throat. But it was a spasm. He was already dead.

The silence after the frenzy of noise and activity was almost painful. Then Mary stirred and swore at the pain from the bullet wound that had scored her back from the left shoulder the length of her shoulder blade. John was unhurt, as was Pamela Chan. Adam had a bullet through his forearm, missing the bones luckily. Donny and Abby were both bruised from the encounter with the Russian in the kitchen, who had reacted with a Sabatier knife. When challenged, he had hurled the tray at them and snatched up the knife to attack. Two bullets from Donny's suppressed automatic were needed to stop him. Abby had caught the tray in her midriff and would be likely to carry the bruises for some time. She had unbalanced Donny who had fallen, luckily holding on to his gun but encountering the corner of the worktop on his way down.

As they looked at each other confirming that they were all alive, from outside came the crash of the shotgun being fired. A second shot followed. Donny turned to go and see what happened, but Isobel walked in carrying the shotgun. "What was that all about? I thought we had all of them here."

"There was a seventh man, in a wheelchair, with a sub-machine gun no less. She tossed a wallet to Adam. "This may interest you," she said.

Adam picked up the wallet with his good hand, and flipped it open. He read the name on the identification care inside. "So he did have a twin brother," he said wonderingly. He bent down and twitched the wallet from the dead man he had called Grigor. "Well, there you are, Georgi. It seems I only put Grigor in a wheelchair, three years ago. And he had a twin brother anyway." He smiled and collapsed onto the floor.

Isobel was there immediately. "Get some cloth for bandages somebody, the poor man is bleeding to death."

The *Swallow* slid quietly through the water, John Ling at the wheel, enjoying the chuckle of the water under the sleek hull. Donny poked his head out of the cabin. "Ready for some food yet?"

"I have been ready for hours. The service on this cruise is terrible."

Mary spoke from below. "Complaints about the service will not be tolerated and they will be punished by short rations and kitchen duty."

Abby appeared with two plates of steaming stew. She grinned at John. "Yours is below. You can make your peace with the chef, personally. Coming, Donny?"

Later, they were all four enjoying the warm evening with the remains of the bottle of wine. Abby said, "I heard from Isobel. Adam is convalescing in the penthouse. She is looking after him until he recovers fully."

Mary said sleepily, "I wonder if he ever will? I don't think what he is suffering from has anything to do with his bullet wound."

"I'm pleased to hear it." Abby said thoughtfully, "For both their sakes, they deserve a little good luck after what they have suffered."

Moored at the Marina del Horta in the Azores, Donny and Abby relaxed on their own in the cockpit of the ketch. The others were ashore for a quiet dinner 'tete-a-tete'.

The silence between them was broken by Abby "We never did get to visit our cousins at the Sorbonne." Donny nodded slowly in silent agreement.

"Another day," he said, obscurely.

Abby sighed. "I have sent an application to Brunel to transfer from Oxford to complete my degree. I decided that I need to keep a closer eye on you now that you are beginning to notice other women."

"Damn!" Donny said. "I have just applied to Oxford for the same reason."

Abby swung round on him. "You haven't surely... You can't ..." She looked him in the eye. "You pig, you had me going there." She threw the cushion at him and dived onto him, causing him to take a serious hold of her so that he could kiss her properly.

When things calmed down again he said." I'm pleased you've decided to change University. I missed you terribly last year. Now I'm looking forward to a little peace and quiet for a change. All this cloak and dagger stuff is all very well but it plays hell with my love life."

The End
(of this episode)

David O'Neil

David O'Neil

Artist and Photographer David O'Neil started writing seriously with a series of Highland guide books. His boyhood ambitions were to fly an aeroplane, and sail a boat. As a boy he and his family were bombed out of their home in London.

He learned to fly with the RAF during his National Service. He started sailing boats while serving in the Colonial Police, in Nyasaland (Malawi). He spent 8 years there, before returning to UK. Since then he lived in southern England where he became a management consultant, for over twenty years. He returned to live in Scotland in 1980, and became a tour guide in1986. He started writing in 2006, the first guide book being published in 2007. A further two have been published since. He started writing fiction in 2007 and has now written five full length novels. He has a collection of short stories in publication at present.